Destined

By
Shani Fenderson

Destined

By
Shani Fenderson

www.shanifenderson.com
www.myspace.com/mayhousepress
www.twitter.com/maylodi
www.facebook.com/mayhousepress

Destined

Published by May House Press & Publications, LLC.
Copyright © 2010 by Shani Fenderson
Cover photography by: Eye Soul Photography
Cover design and illustration by: Shani Fenderson

ISBN-10: 0-615-35180-8
ISBN-13: 978-0-615-35180-3
LCCN: 2009909641
First Printing April 2010
Printed in the United States of America
10 9 8 7 6 5 4 3 2 1

This is a work of fiction. It is not meant to depict, portray, or represent any particular real persons. Names, characters, places, and incidents are either the product of the author's imagination or are used fictitiously, and any resemblance to actual persons living or dead, business establishments, events or locales are entirely coincidental.

May House Press & Publications, LLC.
Troup, Texas 75789

There is no testimony without a test........

Chapter
1

Rebeccah Elise Carpenter

I've traveled quite often in my life. Part of the time in my world journeys, I would partake in business ventures. Other times, the extravagant times, you could say that I would travel for the excitement and adventure in seeing and doing something new. I've noticed the good things, had many challenges, and even come across a few disasters. Through it all, I have missed something. I guess that's why I travel often, trying to find myself. You see, I have been a loner all of my life, no brothers nor sisters that I know of; who knows what my father could have gotten into during his prime. He and my mom divorced when I was ten and I never forgave him for that. Being shipped from one state to the next during summer holidays with him, or shall I say being in his way, has taught me that men are not always what we wish them to be for us.

Somehow I feel women are burdens in their world. Men use women and have no care for the woman's feelings. Meanwhile, in the process, she literally is used up. So as you can see, I my friend am now a loner and I kind of like it that way. Don't get me wrong, a woman of my place does get lonely every now and again. I feel if I occupy my mind with other things, exciting adventurous things, I know I will be just fine.

People keep me humble and my line of work keeps me busy. I just don't have time for unnecessary relationships. I really hate that word; relationship. Humph! I have not related with anyone lately, especially a man. Call it what you may, but being single in my opinion is the only way to go. I don't have to worry about anyone checkin' up on me every now and again or no silly arguments about who calls me at all times of the day. Heck, I'm a businesswoman. I constantly get calls during odd hours, so jealousy shouldn't be an issue with a man who I decide to share my life with. I am a woman in charge and on the go. Right now at this very moment for me to find a man who is suitable for my mood changes, is not what I am looking for. I am happy being me; smart, single, sexy, headstrong, and in charge.

Rebeccah's friend Kathy did not quite understand why she, *Ms. Headstrong* sister Reebie, took the comfort in being such a loner. It was hard to fathom a woman with so much beauty and talent wanting to be single and not date at all. Kathy never quite understood how an able body, fine as all get out kind of a woman, did so much traveling by herself.

"Girl, I just don't see how you do it," Kathy stated while looking at Rebeccah wanting to know why every successful woman, especially her dear friend, didn't have a man on her side.

"What do you mean," Rebeccah asked not really wanting to go into the same conversation that she always had with Kathy. "Do what?"

"How can you go to all of these exquisite uppity places by yourself and not have a beau on your arm to share the excitement with?"

Rebeccah never really gathered why someone would want her to be tied down. Her life was her work and work alone. A man, to her, would come into the picture and completely ruin her lifestyle. There would be less traveling across the globe, long drawn out contracts which consisted of rigorous challenges that she loved to take head on, and late nights at the office looking for new talent. She did not contemplate the idea of dating one bit. Just the idea of her being in a relationship made her feel miserable.

"Girl it is as easy as baking a cake," she said while getting ready to break down her rules of traveling solo as if she were literally baking a cake. "All you have to do is enjoy the moment. Live completely in that wonderful moment, of course by yourself, and not worry about what you are missing or think you may be missing."

Rebeccah wanted to reiterate the fact that being solo was healthy and tasty as the invisible finished five-layer cake she pretended to make on the table.

"Whatever, woman," Kathy retorted and smacked her lips to prove her point in return. "You are completely lying to yourself."

"No I am not," Rebeccah said without hesitation while reminiscing of her life alone. "I enjoy the cruises, five-star hotels, and the sites just fine by myself."

"You're *lying*, Rebeccah," she said while giving her the playful evil eye as if to say *whatever*.

"I am not. There are way too many people in this world who do not have the things that I am able to buy, see, and do. For me a man is neither something that I need to harbor on nor what I want right now. I am a single professional woman who has the money and the time to do it all by myself, with no distractions whatsoever."

"See. Ya lying."

"You know what," Rebeccah said frustrated with her

friend.

    She didn't want to admit that what was being said was a little right. At times for Rebeccah it did get a little lonely. However, when she added up all the wonderful things that she had seen and encountered in the world, somehow she knew that she had nothing to be lonely about. She felt completely blessed to be able to do all from her accomplishments.

    Rebeccah started her record company from nothing and was now number twenty five on the Forbes 100 list of the youngest richest women in the world. She had everything she could ever desire. Her life was a good thing. She figured by the time that she was thirty she would have settled down and found the one to build her life with. Three years had gone by and she was still doing it on her own. Nonetheless, with the trifling brothers she would come across everyday, she knew that that dream was just not going to happen anytime soon. Thirty-three was a big number. She knew she had to move forward without looking back. Rebeccah's motto was, 'if he aint seriously in it in the beginning, then why even bother with carrying a man along who half steps.' Life seemed to be too short and she was not getting any younger. Playing games and towing extra baggage around was definitely out of the question.

    In her line of work she would run into all types of brothers. Once there was a man, if she could call him that, in his mid forties who was still trying to pursue his dream of being a famous R&B singer. Every few minutes he would belt out her name in song, creating lyrics that would make Rebeccah want to curl in a corner to hide.

    "*Reeeebeccccaaaaaaaaah*, I wanna *loooovvvvvvvvveeeee* you, More than you will *evvvvvvvverrrrrr* know. I want to hold you *iiiiiiiiin* the snow, just the sound of me saying your name would make you want to curl your....":

    "Ok! Ok! Check please," she finally said to him out

loud pushing her chair from the table.

"You wanna leave me my darl *li li* ling. The night is still young and your heart is cal *li li* ling for me."

Rebeccah walked out of the restaurant before she could hear anymore. She could only imagine seeing herself with him for *eter ni ta ta ty*. That was definitely out of the question.

On another occasion, she met this man who seemed to be perfect in every way. He drove a nice car, was well dressed, wonderful job, but everything that came out of his mouth was a lie. He had forgotten that Rebeccah knew just about everyone in the entertainment world. He claimed that he was a backup dancer. In actuality, he was a male wanna be stripper who had his break-out performance on the internet.

Rebeccah understood that she didn't have time for any nonsense, lies, or games. Everything had to be up front, to the point, and strictly straight forward. If no one could come with anything correct in the beginning, business or even love for that matter, she would read him like a book from front to back without any questions. Her second motto was for herself and others, "be real, be you, nothing more and nothing less."

Brian Foster

I have come to the realization that your past will follow you wherever you go. No matter how many times you try to run away from it, it still haunts you. I have been trying not to be the old me. I want to change, heck I try to change as often as I can, but something keeps pulling me back. The old life was comfortable. It always has been for me. No one lets me down and I know what to expect from the streets. It is what it is and will never change. It's always home for me. At times I just feel safe.

Brian Foster had been a man of the cloth just about all of his adult life. However, the expectations of those around him seemed to be overwhelming at times, especially from those who had been down with him from day one. Growing up on the East End of Tennessee was a condition made for most to have to hustle on the streets. Brian's friends that grew up with him, mainly his boy Mike, would never let him lose track of where he came from. Mike constantly reminded Brian of the life that he once lived before theology school and he would never let the past stay where it belonged, in the past.

"Say man, have you seen any honeys at that new spot that you at?" Mike asked while taking a sip of rum and coke standing next to the bar.

"New honeys? You say it as if it's some kind of club or something, '*spot*.' I aint there for that man!" Brian responded feeling a little bored with trying to still satisfy Mike's memory of the past.

"Yes you are man," Mike alleged trying to prove to Brian once again that he was a liar. "You started out saying back in the day you could not wait being in a pulpit so that you could find the one or one hundred and one of your dreams."

"Man *stop* playing," Brian said a little aggravated.

"Playing I aint, man. That came directly from yo' mouth."

"I must have been tired, studying, or something."

"Nope, man how you gone forget? You was sippin' on some Bacardi watchin' a video in the dorms when you said it. You don't remember that night? I do cause honey in that video was…"

"Yo Mike you full of it," Brian said stopping him before he went any further.

"Nah man, I think you full of it."

"Besides, I don't mess with God man."

"You don't, huh?" Mike reiterated while beginning to remind Brian of his life in theology school. "Well, what about the time when you met that sistah up in VA?"

"Don't go there brother," Brian retorted beginning to be even more frustrated with his friend.

"Nah seriously!"

"Nah seriously don't, man. The past was the past so let it stay there."

"Hell, her past will be with you for twenty years or until you die!"

"See, why you gotta talk about that, man?"

"Brian, the truth is the truth brah, and *it* shall set you free. Aint that what you be saying," Mike said while looking up towards the sky and waving his hands for mercy. "Besides, how is he anyway?"

"He's cool. He just doesn't want anything to do with me is all."

"Well I hear that, man," Mike whispered while trying to console Brian after rehashing the past. "My son is doin' fine, but that mother of his is another story."

"Bringing up old news is what you about, huh?" Brian glanced at his old friend regretting the trip to California, and his past.

"Nah, Brian. I am just a realist and life is real. All that mumbo jumbo you be feeding to them folks is a bunch of…"

"Man Hold up, hold up. Don't play like that."

"All I'm sayin' is, you can't run from who you are. Ya feel me?"

"Nah you can't, but you can change," Brian answered

sounding hopeful that one day his boy Mike would understand his change in becoming a Preacher instead of another man on the block.

"Are you changing?" Mike asked sarcastically.

"What kind of question is that, man?"

"Well if you were changing, you wouldn't have been ready to come to the club tonight?"

"I just came 'cause...."

"'Cause of what brah, to save some souls?"

"Man if I didn't know you I, would clock you one," Brian replied while being reminded that he was truly not completely perfect; especially since he was standing in a hip hop club next to a bar. Wrong was wrong, even if he did have a glass of soda in his hand.

"Nah, you can pray for me is what you can do. While you at it, pray for yourself and that fine *sistah* right there," Mike half heartedly responded while eyeing a short petite cocoa brown sister in a tight blue dress walking towards the bar.

"Say baby, what's your name is?" he asked while gawking at her.

Brian began to ask himself again why he was even there. He knew that someone could possibly notice him. There was no way he could explain why he of all people, a Preacher, was standing by a bar in a club with a glass in his hand. He became even more paranoid hoping a fight would not break out seeing how he noticed that the people around him seemed to be a little immature, even his boy Mike. The idea of being noticed had bothered him so much that he started sweating and getting a little nauseated. He then relaxed when he thought that maybe no one would recognize him in the dimly lit club that was several thousand miles away from his hometown.

He and Mike had flown out to San Diego for the weekend just to get away. But it never failed; a person would always recognize him when he traveled. Whenever Brian called himself getting away from his home church and community, he would tend to run into someone that knew of him or had seen him on a billboard, television, or newspaper back in Tennessee.

"Say Brian, this here is Nacole," Mike said with the unfamiliar woman by his side snapping Brian out of his moment of fear. "Nacole this is mah boy Brian."

"Please to meet you," Brian said noticing her smile then at how she was scantily dressed like a lady of the evening.

"And you, too." Nacole smiled while holding a drink in one hand and reaching out to shake Brian's hand with the other.

"Have I seen you before?" she asked

Brian again thought to himself how this scenario never failed and wondered why he would always put himself in the same situation.

"Nah I don't think so," he said while slightly turning his head.

"Well, you seem so familiar," she replied trying to figure out where or how she possibly knew him.

"Enough of the small talk baby," Mike said changing the subject. "Let's get out and dance."

"Ok, but let me tell my girl over there," she looked while pointing to a dark corner in the club.

Both Brian and Mike looked towards the corner where she was pointing and really didn't notice anyone of significance sitting there.

"You don't mind keeping her company do you, Brian?"

"Not at all. It would be an honor," he said while eyeing Mike as if to say let's go man, but he knew that wouldn't happen.

"Good 'cause it's her birthday today and she alone

right about now. She doesn't date much."

"*Wow another sister with problems,*" Brian questioned to himself while looking up to the heavens for answers. He decided not to even ask above because he knew he was in the wrong. *"When will it ever end"* he murmured to himself.

"Beccah, you have a call on line two," Candice called over the intercom.

"Who is it?" asked Rebeccah.

"It's Terry Hunt and your two o'clock is here."

"Ok give me just a minute."

Rebeccah had been waiting for Terry's call all day. Terry had been a close friend of hers since they attended college together. He was her best and only male gay friend. He knew exactly what to say and when to say it, a sharp tongue that could pierce through leather because he knew how to take care of business. No one ever tried to cross

Terry the wrong way but when they would, Rebeccah enjoyed watching how he was straightforward with them. It was poetry in motion or at least a boxing match with the contender not knowing what hit him. What she enjoyed the most about Terry was he would always be right there for her whenever she was down. He would find a way to make her feel at ease.

Terry was musically inclined, just as much as Rebeccah. His heart and love for music was always with the church, completely opposite of her. She loved the way he would play a piano as if the world were coming to an end. It shocked Rebeccah and everyone else when he came out of the closet two years prior. Everyone always suspected that he was gay, even if at one point in his life he had dated women. Oddly enough Terry was even engaged, that was until he met some brother at a music workshop in Dallas.

Each year he would go to several music directors' workshops and the stories that Terry would bring back to Rebeccah made her realize that the meetings were not just for sheet music, it was a place for in between the sheet making music. He explained to her that the events were just like a meat market for single and married men to hook up with their perspective beaus. At a particular seminar in Dallas, two weeks prior to Terry's wedding day, he decided to call Rebeccah up with not a good story for his wife to be.

"Reebie, what's up lady?" Terry said sounding a little puzzled.

"Nothing much. Are you ready?" Rebeccah asked excited for her friend.

"For what?" he asked sounding preoccupied.

"What do you mean for what? Your biggest day is about to arrive and you seem to have forgotten all about it."

"Oh about that," he finally answered after still contemplating about something or someone else. "No baby, never that. I have just had a lot on my mind is all."

"So tell me about it," Rebeccah curiously asked wanting to know what had a hold of her best friends mind.

"Not just yet. I still have some things I have to do."

"Oh last minute groom stuff?"

"Something *like* that."

"Gee, you sure do sound happy about the entire thing," she said seeing that he would not budge. She suspected he had cold feet and didn't want to upset him.

"Oh no, hun. I'm happy. Happy as a lark," he said sounding unconvincing.

"Come on Terry, I know you better than that."

"I know you do love but I was calling you about something else."

"What could be more important than your wedding?"

"Look lady, enough with the twenty-one questions

already," he snapped. "I have a question for you, actually a favor."

"What kind of favor?" she asked a little worried.

"I need you to look up someone's information for me."

"You have me playing private eye again?"

"Not really. Can you do it or not?" he demanded.

"Dang, why you so hostile?"

"It's important," he said sounding desperate.

"Well, for you to sound so serious about it, I guess I can."

"Good. You still have that friend that works at the tax office right?"

"Yes."

"I can't tell you all the information over the phone, but I am going to get back with you on it when I talk with you again later."

"Not a problem. You know you really have me worried now."

"Don't be worried, love. I gotta go but I will talk with you later."

"Ok, cya."

"Bye, boo."

Rebeccah knew Terry was up to something. She didn't know how major it had been until he had her look up some female's information that was not his fiancés. Instead, it turned out to be his new lover's wife. His lover at the time, Keith ended up leaving his wife because she was cheating on him. To make matters worse, the person she was messing with was of course not a man, but another woman.

After that, Rebeccah figured that dating and marriages didn't mean anything anymore by today's standards. Rebeccah believed that everyone who was in a relationship was going through extra marital affairs. She felt that if anyone who was in a relationship didn't straighten up and fly right, they would end up in hell.

"Beccah you still have that call on line two, sweetie," Candice said bringing Rebeccah back from her reminiscing.

"Girl, it has been busy in here," Rebeccah replied while fidgeting with paperwork on her desk.

"I know. Tell me about it." Candice responded while walking out of the door and back to her desk.

"Hello, Terry," Rebeccah chimed to her friend who had been waiting on the line for ten minutes.

"Hello *Ms.* Carpenter. How are you this fine day?"

"Just fine and you?"

"Tre bien!" Terry answered in his not so smooth accent. "So what are you doing this evening, you have plans?"

"Not necessarily," she said while she looked out of her office window noticing how beautiful the day was. "Why, what's up?"

"I just wanted to really see a sexy old friend."

"I know it has to be more than that."

"How you figure darling?" he asked coyly.

"Because of the way you came at me all sexy when we know I am not your type yesterday, today, or tomorrow."

"It's because you *are* sexy darling. Sexy and fierce! You bring it out in me," he chuckled.

Rebeccah could hear him snapping his fingers in the background and it made her giggle imaging her friend being more feminine than her. "Whatever! Actually it is a busy day for me. but we can do lunch tomorrow."

"Lunch! What a shame," Terry responded sounding a little upset by being put on the back burner. "See a brother tries to cook you a meal and you reject him. Now wonder you're still single."

"Being busy has nothing to do with my being single."

"But in fact it does, darling."

"And how is that?"

"You are so busy taking care of everyone else's

problems, signing contracts, looking for new artist, singing, rapping, whatever it is you do in your little cubicle, and you tend to forget about you."

"I don't forget about me and besides, it's *not* a cubicle. It's a corner office with my name on the front of the building, thank you very much."

"Whatever, babygirl. All I'm saying is that you need to love you and allow someone else to love you as well before you end up tired, old, and alone."

"I am not alone," she reminded Terry, "that's why I got you."

"Yeah your tiny little cubicle, and me" he said jokingly.

"*Anywayz,* I have an appointment now so can we do lunch tomorrow or what?"

"Oh now you want to be feisty about it. Forget it then."

"No, no Terry I'm sorry," She apologized after realizing how abrupt she was. "It's just been busy here."

"Too busy to even talk to the *only* man in your life?"

"Ok see you know what? Bye boy!"

"Call me when you get home."

"I will," she confirmed.

"I love you."

"Love you, too," she replied and then hung up.

Rebeccah had missed hearing those three words at times. She missed hearing a brother, especially one who was not gay, metro sexual or down low, telling her that he loved her. She knew she didn't have time to harbor on the thought and found herself saying out loud, "Oh well, life goes on." Rebeccah did feel alone, but for the time being work was more important.

"Candace, send in my two o'clock please," Rebeccah called through the intercom.

"Yes ma'am."

"So Brian, how did it go with your lady friend last night?" Mike asked while they took a seat at the terminal gate waiting for their flight to be called.

"*Go*? It didn't go anywhere, man," Brian replied sounding upset that his friend dared to ask him a question that would insinuate that he was promiscuous.

"Man come on now," Mike said after nudging Brian.

"I'm serious, man. You really think that I don't want to be that way anymore huh?"

"Nope I don't. But check this though on the real, she had body brah. You gotta be a fool not to try nothing."

"What does *body* have to do with her heart?"

"Everything!"

"And why is that?"

"Because, man. You never would have come out here on this trip to begin with if you were just looking for a heart," Mike claimed once again reminding Brian that he was not perfect.

"Man I needed a break," he reassured Mike.

"A break from what? The sister shouting on the first row?"

"Nah man, I just needed to think some things out."

"Well while you were thinking, I was working."

"Mike spare the details brother."

"Spare you the details, man what!" he said eyeing Brian up and down. "Are you getting a little soft on me now?"

"Nope, not soft."

"A little fruity on me?"

"No not that either, man. You just wouldn't understand."

"Yes I would. Try me."

"It's just that I am missing my rib."

"Oh man you want some ribs? I heard that they got this rib spot in Skyline somewhere," Mike said pointing towards the airport doors while grinning.

"See that's what I am saying, man," Brain said upset because his friend did not comprehend what he meant by missing his rib. "Forget it."

"Nah I'm just playing, Brian. I'm all ears."

"Man, nah-nah forget it," he said contemplating on sharing how he felt to his boy from the block.

"Would you tell me? I promise no more jokes, but a brother here is hungry, especially after last night. Man last night, I don't know about you, but for me it was on point."

Mike went on one of his rampages. He never took the time to hear Brian out, which really upset him at times. Mike acted like he cared but in actuality the story or tales would always end up about him. Brian didn't want to change back to what he used to be, a street hustler. He was better at being a Preacher. He thought for a second that maybe he was getting a little soft, but then realized that he couldn't be soft. His job required him to be hard. He had to be a strong masculine type of man who knew the answers to everything. That was part of his calling.

Brian could tell what someone's next move would be before they would even take it. That was the case especially when it came to his boy, Mike. He already knew that Mike would make a joke about something that would be serious to Brian and his life. In fact, Brian also knew that Mike would turn the entire story around and switch everything to where *he* would be the topic of conversation. Brian new he needed Mike around though. He had to love the guy like his own blood, especially since they had gone through so much together.

"Brian. Brian," Mike said.

"'Sup?"

"You are not listening to me, man."

"Nah I heard you."

"It was crazy how that girl knew you though."

"What do you mean she knew me?"

"She said she remembered you from somewhere," Mike said laughing.

"And?" Brian said feeling upset all over again.

"*And,* she saw you in a commercial when she was on a business trip in Tennessee. She even gave me the name of that spot where you be preachin' at and everything."

"Here we go again, man. Is she from back home?"

"Nah man it aint even like that. You don't have to worry about that one bit. I just promised her I would keep in touch. Besides man, she isn't from Tennessee at all. She's from around this way."

"Good, I can't mess up my reputation."

"Mess it up? If these women and men knew what you were about before you even stepped foot in a church, they would flip out."

"Yeah, but the past is the past. People change."

"And like I told you yesterday, the past will always pop up. You can never run from it."

"Man I heard you, I heard you," Brian said while the lady at the gate started to call out the boarding information. "Let's go, man. I think that's our flight they are calling."

Chapter
2

"Reebie, when are you going with me to church?"
Terry asked concerned for his friends well being.

"Church! What is that?" Rebeccah asked while
sipping some champagne.

"Come on now. You know that you are only
successful because of one Supreme Being and not because of
education or hard work," he reminded her while pointing up
towards the sky.

"I know that, but I don't need some old school pimp
telling me that. I can read my Bible on my own," she
contorted.

"Girl, stop playing with God and His workers," he
reiterated while looking for support from Kathy who was
sitting across the table.

"Workers? Right! There are way too many heathens
up in the church today for me *anywayz*," she said while taking
a bite of her Chicken Parmesan.

"I think you need some serious praying for," he
glanced at her then looked to the skies and back at her again.
"Besides miss thing, church is not just about the wrong things
you just said, it's about the Lord and you possibly finding a
man there."

"You're funny, Terry," Rebeccah chuckled.

"Girl he is serious," Kathy finally spoke. "You may find you a good man in the church, he did."

"Kathy stop," Terry said while pointing at her. "I met my friend at an event with church members, not at the church itself, sweetie."

"Well, the both of you cannot change a sister's mind. I will go when it is time for me to go to church. Me and God already have a deal," Rebeccah stated.

"And what kind of deal is that?" Terry asked looking her up and down.

"Yeah, what kind of deal is that, Beccah," chimed Kathy.

"Well to the both of you, it's between God and me, no outsiders," she said while still eating her meal.

"All I know is, you need to make it known that you do acknowledge the Lord," Kathy said.

"I do acknowledge Him, Kathy," Rebeccah answered starting to get annoyed.

"When?!" they both asked in unison.

"Why are you two hounding me? We are here for lunch."

"Yeah you're right, Terry. She aint gonna change," Kathy responded while looking at Terry and pointing at Rebeccah as if she was not even at the table.

"Nah, Kathy. She is just straight and narrow with nowhere to go," he pointed forward with his knife.

"Yeah and if she keeps it up, it will be to a fiery furnace," Kathy replied seriously.

"Man! What is with you two talking around me like I am not even here?"

"Nothing. We just want you to be happy," replied Terry.

"Yeah happy and saved is all," added Kathy while taking a bit of her salad.

"For your *information* I am saved," Rebeccah

confirmed.

"Really?! Have you ever been baptized?" asked Kathy.

"Uhm, what is this Bible study or something?" Rebeccah stated.

"Well have you?" Terry asked.

"Yes!"

"When?" Kathy asked waiting for a response from her friend who was looking around the restaurant for a way out.

"When I was ten, why?"

"You are not asking the questions here. We are," Terry explained.

"When was the last time she said she attended a church? Since you were ten?!" Kathy looked at both Terry and Rebeccah then took a bite of her salad. "Right, it is time."

"Wait, wait, wait, wait a minute. You two almost had me with the guilt thing, but you guys are up to something. Something is not right with this little charade you are pulling here."

"What in the world would that be Rebeccah Elise Carpenter?" Terry asked.

"Oh see, now you using my entire name," Rebeccah said seeing through what they were trying to play. "You two think you are slick. Kathy, Kathy girl you know you are hearing me over there trying to hide behind your napkin."

"What is it?" Kathy asked looking a little puzzled.

"Don't say a thing Kathy," Terry said looking at her trying to stop her from breaking under pressure. "Don't let her break you down. Be strong sister..."

"Kathy, what is it girl?" Rebeccah asked in her calm but deceiving voice. "What do you two have up your sleeve?"

"It wasn't my idea," she started.

"Girl I told you not to say anything," Terry said upset because he knew that she could no longer hold the secret.

"And you Mr. Terrance Tramain Hunt," Rebeccah

said while getting ready to read Terry like a book.

"What? I didn't do a thing," he said trying to look away.

"One of ya'll is about to confess before I make a scene in the middle of this restaurant."

"Too late," they both retorted,.

Rebeccah realized how loud she had gotten but by then it was too late and she was upset. Both Terry and Kathy rarely stressed religion to Rebeccah, especially like the way they had just approached her. She knew that they were up to something because they always tended to gang up on her when they wanted her to do something their way. It was a game they loved playing, but Rebeccah would never fall for it.

"So who is going to tell me?" Rebeccah asked with her arms folded and the knife in her hand.

"You tell her," Terry said.

"Nah you tell her," Kathy said trying to get Terry to tell all.

"I am not saying anything."

"But it was your idea. You tell her."

"Man will one of you tell me," Rebeccah annoyingly replied stopping the verbal match they had going.

Terry took a sip of water before he began telling all, "Ok. Well see, what had happened was, there is this revival going on in a few weeks, and we kind of uhm...."

"We!? You mean you kind of," Karen abruptly interrupted as to not be accused of anything.

"It doesn't matter, ya'll. What is it?"

"Well I kind of signed you up to do a solo," Terry said in fear for what wrath Rebeccah was about to send his way.

"A what?! A solo Terry! Are you serious? Come on man!"

"But Reebie, baby, you have been blessed with a

voice sweetie."

"Kathy, and you knew about this?"

"Uhm just a little," she said afraid of how far Rebeccah would go since she knew that her reply was about to be the beginning of danger.

"How long ago did you know?" she asked while standing up with her hand on her purse.

"A month," she said while taking a sip of water.

"A month! You guys have lost your minds and who's to say that I do not have anything planned for that day?"

"You don't," they said together.

"What do you mean *I* don't?"

"We already checked with Candice and you are free. She pinned you in and everything," Terry said proud of getting the work done without Rebeccah's knowledge.

"I don't believe this. She will be fired and you two are on my list now!"

"What list is that?" Kathy curiously asked.

"I can't stand list!" Rebeccah said while storming out of the restaurant.

"Just let her go," Terry said. "She'll get over it."

"But she was suppose to pay," Kathy said while looking at the bill.

Rebeccah could not believe that they had set her up that way. She had to leave the restaurant because no one ever made plans for her except her. She thought about several reasons why she should not be married. One was making plans without her consent. She lived her life for her and no one else. She didn't have to check in or out. She could leave whenever she felt like it, travel whenever she wanted, all without a man saying that she needed to stay home and take care of the children or cook him a meal.

Rebeccah felt betrayed because the one thing her friends could ever do wrong to her, they did. They had signed her up to do a solo at a church that she never stepped foot in.

She felt that they didn't realize that she was not Christian material. They did not understand that she did not like being tied down to any one church just because she didn't trust the men who ran them? In Rebeccah's eyes, the men that were leaders of the church were at one point *worldly* men. Some of them still used the church as a cover up; at least that's how it looked in her eyes.

"Of all the dirty most conniving things to do to me, I can not believe this," Rebeccah said aloud while she was driving back to her office. She figured they were acting strange for a reason and that something had to have been up. She always had a gut feeling about things, but she didn't know that they would take it as far as they had. She couldn't wait to get back to the office to tell Candice that her services were no longer needed as an employee but the realized that she sent her home early. "I will deal with her tomorrow since it is going to be a long day of work."

———

"Brother Hunt," Brian asked while walking up to Terry who was sitting at the piano going through his sheet music. "Is everything set for the meeting in a few weeks?"

"That it is Pastor," Terry said giving Brian some reassurance.

"I'm just checkin' to make sure everything is together. I know you got something wonderful lined up," he smiled.

"I won't let the Lord, or you down, brother," smiled Terry while looking to the heavens.

"Amen, brother. Amen," Brian said shacking Terry's hand.

Brian loved it when the people he had chosen would come through and work together as a team. The up and coming event would be the first meeting that Brian had ever put together in his time as being a Pastor. He had noticed how everything worked when he was an Assistant Pastor for five years. Being the head pastor meant more than just observing, Brian had to be hands on and wanted everything for revival to be right, especially since it would be simulcast on television and radio. He was really anxious and excited, which is why he was so thankful for having such great help.

Brian knew that it would be hard to find the right people on his team for the Lord, but luckily he had been blessed with many talented folk from his church. The only problem he would come across was that so many of the single sisters wanted to help him for the wrong reasons. They would try anything just to be in his life; seeing that he was single. He had come across some nice sisters who at first seemed sincere with their help, but later on down the line he realized that they did favors for him because of his position. They had dreams of being the first lady of the church and standing by his side. Those types of women were attracted to the dream and lifestyle instead of the life for Christ. Brian could see through it and knew it by the obvious ways they treated him. Nothing was genuine and he was beginning to think that a help meet did not exist for him.

One sister, who claimed she loved the Lord and wanted to get to know Brian a little more, had invited him over to her family's home for dinner. Her family treated him nice; she even went to the extent of bringing him meals every Sunday. She also knew some of the people he had gone to Theology Seminar with. However, when she would be around him in private, her entire demeanor would change. She was overly aggressive towards him and touchy feely when no one else would be around. He decided to leave her alone. When he would see her at church he saw right through the Amen's and Hallelujah's because she would still wink at him while he would be in the pulpit preaching. He loved the attention, but he didn't want to have any of the wrong attention following in behind him.

Brian despised the fact that most of the female parishioners would take things to the extreme, especially one sister who had written him a letter of the things that she wanted him to do for her; and to him. Nothing on the list or letter that she had written had anything to do with church business. Instead, she wanted to be with him alone on her own accord. She left nothing to the imagination and it showed him how disrespectful she was towards herself. He thought that women were just as bad as men when they saw something that they wanted. All he was able to do for those women who had the wrong intentions was to leave them alone, pray for them, and ask the Lord to guide him to his destiny.

"Hello, Pastor Foster," a young lady said while walking into his office without even knocking.

She was a prime example of what Brian disliked when it came to women who tried excessively hard to be by his side.

"Say, Sister Walker," he said to her thinking that she should have been called street walker lady of the evening. He knew that he shouldn't judge anyone, but this woman standing before him made him judge her quite often. She would wear the shortest skirts that were made with as little material as possible. The other problem that Brian was irritated with her about was that she would always want to drop something on the floor and pick it up in front of him. The routine never failed. Brian was also ashamed of her because of the blouses that she wore. They were always cut too low, overly revealing, and should have been banned in fifty-one states. Especially Sin City.

"Yes, Sister Walker. How are you doing?"

"Oh please, Brian. No formalities," Lesha said moving closer to her target. "I told you many times before. Enough with the formalities, it's Lesha."

"I know. I know, Sister Walker," he said wanting her

to realize that he was not interested in her at all. "I just think it is more appropriate if I called you correctly."

"Speaking of calling," she said remembering something important, "you never returned my call this weekend."

"Oh. I didn't get a chance to check my messages remember," he said at least being honest, "I was out of town."

"Oops," she said while knocking a stapler off of Brian's desk. "I didn't mean to knock that off your desk. Let me get that."

Brian thought the routine never failed and she should stop if she knew how silly she looked. "That's ok, sister. I'll get it," he said while walking to pick up the stapler off of the floor before she started revealing more then what was already noticeable.

"Not a problem, *honey*. Let me."

He had wondered if she knew how tacky she looked and that she was nowhere a thought in his mind or heart. "How may I help you today?" he said a little disgusted with the charade she kept pulling on him.

"Well, I came by to tell you that I had performed a solo this past weekend and I have a tape of it if you wanted to hear," she said pulling out a tape from her purse.

"I actually don't have time at the moment, but you can leave it here for later," he said going back to sit in his chair.

"I wanted to make sure that you got it in your hands and heard it to tell me how much you like my voice."

"Oh a persistent one are you? Gotta love it."

"A sister must try you know. Besides, I wanted you to pass it on to Brother Hunt. He can probably use my expertise during the revival."

"Have you tried taking it to him yourself?"

"I have, but every time I get near him, he seems to

walk in the opposite direction as if he never did see me. Funny man you know."

Brian wondered if she understood why he walked away from her. She should have known that every man was not interested in her, especially a gay one.

"He has been pretty busy. I will make sure he gets it though."

"That's your copy," Lesha grinned. "I have one for him, too. Are you sure you don't want to listen to it right now?"

"I wish I could, sister, but I am tremendously busy."

"How about over dinner?"

"Wow, you never stop. It's good seeing sisters so dedicated."

"Dedicated is what I truly am," Lesha said raising her skirt to sit on the edge of his desk. "It seems like you will never find out will you?"

"Excuse me?"

"I mean, it seems that you never take the time to figure out my..."

"Brother Foster, I have something for you," Sister Jenkins said walking in right on time.

Brian thought to himself how wonderful it was to be saved by the bell. "Yes, Sister Jenkins?"

"Hello, Sister Walker."

"Hhm!" she frowned and stood up. "*Mrs.* Jenkins."

"You look very attractive today," Sister Jenkins said eyeing Lesha up and down.

"At least someone noticed," Lesha said looking Brian's way. "Why thank you, sister. Call me ok, Brian!"

"Will do, Sister. Will do."

"That sister is a hand full aint she," replied Sister Jenkins who was heavy set motherly woman.

"Yes ma'am. That she is."

"I saw that you were in danger so I decided to help

you out."

"Thank you again."

"God bless you, son 'cause you are going to need it around that child."

"God bless you, too." Brian was again thankful for having people on his team, especially someone like Sister Jenkins. At times he would call her Momma Jenkins because she would take care of him when he first came to the church. He noticed that his team players would always step in when he was in a clutch and take care of the rest of his plays for him. He thought to himself, *"God is good, God is good."*

———

Rebeccah did not know why she had still been upset with her friend's actions the previous day. She knew that it had been awhile since she had been to church. Any church for that matter. Her friends were right. Rebeccah figured that she was okay when she tithed like everyone else. However, she hadn't stepped foot in a church in years. The closest thing she had gotten to a church was by watching Television. She would view them long enough to get a mailing address but never really paid any attention to the sermons. Every now and again she would call the prayer lines. While being placed on hold she figured she should hang up because all of her request would be about herself and no one else. She felt it was beginning to be too selfish, so she stopped calling the prayers lines altogether.

Rebeccah never knew how to think about other people because the bottom line, in her eyes, had been about her future and well being only. She figured she had been a little harsh on her friends. They always had her back whenever she needed them and she hardly ever let them down. She was just upset at the way they went about changing her schedule and putting her on the spot. She missed out on enjoying and finishing her favorite dish. She believed that all they had to do was just ask her and she would have at least thought about the idea, but never would have said yes exactly.

"Rebeccah?"

"Yes, Candice."

"Someone sent these to you."

"Does it have a card?"

"I think so," she said while looking for one. "Here it is."

"Just put them over there," Rebeccah said reaching out for the card and pointing towards the coffee table in the office for Candice to place the flowers on.

"Is there anything else I can get for you?"

"No, honey, that's fine. Oh wait," Rebeccah said reminding herself about Candice's mistake.

"What's up?"

"The next time someone wants to make any changes with my schedule other than me, be sure to come to me first no matter who it is."

"Yes ma'am. Sorry about that."

"Not a problem."

"It's just they were so persistent about it."

"I can understand those two being that way."

"Besides that, the Preacher there is very nice."

"You attend church there, too?"

"Yeah, and I have heard you sing so many times before so I figured everyone should be blessed by your voice."

"Why thank you, Candy. Just remember no more changes without me first."

"Gotcha," she said walking out of the office.

Rebeccah had never known that so many people had paid that much attention to her singing. She did plenty of fill-in work and back-up singing when some of the other artist would not show up. She never thought in a million years she would have to sing in a church, especially now with her lifestyle. As a child she would do all kinds of singing in the junior choir, from leads, to alto or soprano, even a little praise dancing. She thought back and remembered that the only reason why she was so active in the church as a child was because her mother forced her to be. Rebeccah was now free from all of that, and didn't think she should change now. "Maybe I should," she said to herself. "It wouldn't hurt me to do something for my best friends."

Terrence was always there for her, now would not be the time for her to be so selfish. Rebeccah looked around the office contemplating on calling Terrence. She dialed his number after thinking about the joy she did have as a youth experiencing church.

"T-bone."

"Oh the lady of the hour."

"Look," she replied before he continued on. "I'm sorry for all the drama. You know how I can get."

"Yes dear," he said knowing that Rebeccah would call back and apologize. She could never stay mad for over two days with him. He clocked her timing just right. "I know how you do, girl. So you got the flowers, huh?"

"That I did," she said looking at the beautiful bouquet that her friend sent to her, being thankful for him knowing her ways.

"Nice aren't they?"

"Yes. You know they are my favorite, right?"

"We know darling. We know."

Rebeccah did not beat around the bush any longer for her time was always precious, everything to the point, and sometimes frivolous was not in her vocabulary; especially when she was about to make a change within herself.

"Look.. I am still upset with the two of you, but I will go ahead and sing something."

"Praise God! Praise God!" Terry shouted on the other end of the line.

Rebeccah had forgotten how loud he could be at times. He was seriously a small man with a voice that can tear the roof down, even if he wasn't trying so hard.

"What do you want me to sing, Amazing Grace?" Rebeccah asked not knowing what the latest songs were in church. She did however want her friend to know that at least she was trying.

"Girl, whatever your heart desires. Just even hearing you mention singing a song for the Lord is a blessing in itself. You do remember the words, right?"

"Stop playing, Terry."

"Ok," he said jokingly. "We have rehearsal starting this Saturday at ten."

"Ten! In the morning? This Saturday? I believe I am busy and have something scheduled for that day."

"No you aren't. We had Candice free you up."

"That girl," Rebeccah said getting a little upset again, especially since she told Candice to not change another thing in her schedule.

"Ooops! I wasn't supposed to say that."

"*Anyway*," Rebeccah said brushing off Terrance's last comment. "Saturday at what time?"

"Ten o'clock."

"Hhm, that's kind of early don't you think?"

"It is never too early for the Lord, girl," Terrence said excited again.

"Ok then. If you say so. I'll be there."

"You better be. Praise God!" he said as if speaking to someone other than Rebeccah. "Praise God! I can't wait to tell everyone we have a '*starah*' performing with us at the revival."

"Bye, Terry," Rebeccah said not waiting for her friend to say anything else before she could change her mind. She then hung up.

Chapter
3

Saturday morning had arrived and Rebeccah was ready to make her appearance. She had gotten up three hours ahead of time just to make sure she would be prepared for her day's event. She found a parking space right in front of the old brick building that was home to The Holy Tabernacle of God. While walking up the steps, she realized that it had been a long time since she had been in a church. She drove by the huge church on several occasions, but never did she figure she would be performing there.

As she made it to the doors, Rebeccah hoped that the church would not burn down as soon as she walked through them. She hesitated for a minute while looking around to see if she should leave, but the parking lot begin to fill up with cars. "Shoots! What do I do? Do I pray first? Man this is hard," she said to herself while barely reaching out to open the door.

"Lord, please forgive me for all the wrong I have done and let me walk through these doors without being struck down. Please God, oh please," she said to herself again while grabbing the door handle. Before she composed herself to fully commit, the doors flew open.

"Girl, what are you standing here for," Kathy asked a little startled. "Come on in, aint nothing going to happen to you."

"Kathy, not so loud. I don't want anyone to know that I am a sinner."

"No one cares about that, girl. Just come in. Terry's waiting for you."

While walking past the long pews, Rebeccah felt within herself that it had been a long time since she had the feeling of being in the environment. It was nothing like the churches she had seen on Television. All those childhood memories of the sights, smells of the old church sanctuary, people smiling and singing, made her feel warm inside. Kathy brought her back from her reverie.

"Terry has been waiting for you," Kathy said looking towards their friend who was standing in front of the choir.

"I'm not late am I?"

"No. Right on time. Let's sit here until he introduces you," Kathy said sitting down at the first pew.

If any time would have been a good time, this was definitely not it for Rebeccah. She was too close to the front to make a clean exit. Looking at her friend directing the choir made her remember how talented a man Terry truly was. While her eyes were closed, she listened to the melody, how they were harmonizing, and the words being sung.

Terry was seriously talented and had them working the song. She offered him a job at the studio many years back, but he declined. Not because of working for her, but her type of music was not as he put it, in his best interest. Rebeccah respected him for sticking to his faith and not allowing anything or anyone discourage him from it.

"Girl, you aint going to sleep over there are you?"

"No, I'm just listening. What are they singing 'cause it seems like they are all into the music and doing the bank head bounce like it's the club in here."

"Girl, it's all for the Lord, all for the Lord," Kathy said while pointing to the ceiling.

Rebeccah looked up trying to figure out what her

friend was pointing at wanting to ask her but then realized she better not because the question may have seemed a little foolish. It had really been a long time since she had been inside a church, for a minute it did fell like a club to her. Everyone had been moving and shaking. She even found herself tapping her toes to the beat. Music in the church had changed tremendously. It sounded like the same music that she was pushing out at her label from the beats and the band playing music. The one thing she felt that separated her label from the church choir was there wasn't any cursing and everything was about the Lord. She knew she was a little green, but the music still had the same foundation as her producers would be pushing.

"Beautiful, just absolutely beautiful brothers and sisters," Terrence said bringing Rebeccah back to reality. "I would like to introduce you to a dear friend of mine. She has slipped away from the Lord, but today she is here for Him and Him alone."

Rebeccah thought he didn't have to announce her in that manner, but she couldn't say or do too much because by that time. all eyes were on her. She was in a church building, cursing Terrence would not have been the appropriate thing to do.

"Everyone I would like to introduce you to Rebeccah Elise Carpenter."

"Oh my goodness, Lord. Please do not strike me down," Rebeccah mumbled under her breath. She felt herself getting a little nervous when all the choir members starting clapping their hands saying *"amen"* and *"praise God."*

"Lord is this you trying to tell me something," she mumbled under her breath again. Rebeccah felt like running out before the Lord would strike her down.

"Come on sister. Don't be shy now" Terrance said reaching out for Rebeccah's hand to come join him in the choir stand. "Praise God!"

"Hello everyone," Rebeccah said shyly.

"*Hello sister*," the choir sang in unison.

"Wow, I wasn't expecting that," she said looking like a deer caught in headlights.

"Amen," Terrance said holding Rebeccah's hand. "Sister Carpenter will be blessing us today with Amazing Grace in the key of C, right?"

"Yes," she said still holding on to her friends hand, not wanting to let go.

"Ok, will do it first without the choir," he said looking at her then at the choir.

"Oh! The choirs going to sing this with me?"

"Yes they are. You just start and we will follow you."

"Ok," she said clearing her throat.

"Pastor Foster, here are those papers you wanted to see," said Sister Jenkins.

"Thank you, sister. Is that the choir I hear?"

"Yes sir. that it is."

"Who's the person doing the solo," Brian asked. For some reason he knew that it was not Lesha whaling away. Instead, the voice he heard sounded happy and sad at the same time. Whoever was singing, the soloist knew how to handle her voice, he thought.

"Oh that's one of Brother Hunt's friends, Ms. Carpenter. She really has a beautiful voice," replied Sister Jenkins while turning towards the sound coming from the sanctuary.

"Does she attend services here?"

"Not that I know of, but I can find out if you'd like."

"That would be fine if you don't mind, sister," Brian said while moving out from behind his desk and walking to his office door. "I think I need to go check them out to see if

I noticed her from any of our services."

Brian knew that he had not heard such a wonderful sound coming from the church choir since he had been a minister there. He had known the capabilities of the choir, but this new voice was graceful and soothing to him. The unfamiliar voice had him in a trance; it was so beautiful and strong. He thought whoever this sister was, she was very confident. Even from the notes she reached he knew that she had a beautiful spirit. He made it to the sanctuary standing on the side of the choir stand not wanting to be obvious. Somehow Sister Jenkins was standing by his side, pleased to see that the Pastor was moved. When he saw the beauty standing there before him singing her heart out for the Lord, he felt overwhelmed. She was as beautiful as she sounded, an average height woman that looked like she had much class about her. He could only see the side of her face, all of that didn't matter to him because she captured something in him that he had been missing for so long.

"Sister Jenkins," he finally turned to her and whispered, "What did you say her name was again?"

"Ms. Rebeccah Carpenter," she whispered in return. "She owns the record label Melodic Voices."

"Thanks, Sister Jenkins," he said. Brian felt that her voice was truly melodic and that Ms. Rebeccah was completely blessed by God. He could not wait to speak to her. She was intriguing. Brian realized that he had to be careful because he didn't want anyone to think any ideas about him wanting to meet her. Sometimes he knew that folks in the church could not hold secrets for too long, and with him being single, they watched every move he made like a hawk. He was a man of the cloth and the idea of him thinking about a woman in front of his congregation was not the image he needed to portray with the stranger. For now, his old ways could not be apparent in any way.

"Amen, choir," Brian said clapping his hands after the

choir had finished. "Amen. That was truly beautiful."

"Thank you, Pastor," Terrence said smiling at the approval then turning to the choir. "We are done for today but before we go, Deacon Thomas, can you lead us in prayer, please?"

Brian felt that this was a good opportunity to be next to the lady that moved him. He stood next to her and grabbed her hand.

"Hello," he said finally seeing her head on. Through his eyes he could see that she was more beautiful than anything or anyone he had ever seen before.

"Hi," she said looking at him then looking down a little embarrassed.

She seemed so familiar to him. He wondered how he knew her, if she was someone from the block. Brian even thought that her smile was beautiful. He knew that he was not supposed to be thinking about anything else but God during prayer, but Deacon Thomas tended to take a good hour just to say 'thank you, Father.' Brian knew that the comment in his head was wrong and asked the Lord to forgive him. He began wondering off again thinking about Ms. Rebeccah. The perfume she was wearing smelled just like soft petals on a flower. She seemed so nice. He again asked the Lord to forgive him because his mind should have been completely in prayer.

"Amen," everyone said together after what seemed like an hour prayer.

"Choir," Terrence said trying to get everyone's attention. "Choir, I will see you all next Saturday same time and don't forget we will be starting nightly rehearsals as well."

Terrance looked at Rebeccah making sure she heard every last word and that she would not have an excuse in not making it to the other rehearsals.

"Pastor Foster, I see you have met my dear friend Rebeccah Carpenter," Terrance said discreetly while noticing that they were still holding hands.

"Pleased to meet you, sister," Brian said feeling overwhelmed with emotions.

"You too, Mr. Foster," Rebeccah said then realizing what she had done wrong. "Oops, I mean Pastor Foster, Brother, uhm…" Rebeccah asked the Lord to forgive her in making another mistake while in the Lord's House. She asked that He would not strike her down, especially since she could not call a man of God by the right name.

"No-no, its fine it's just a formality. You can call me Brian."

"Well ok, Brian. You can call me Rebeccah."

"Rebeccah, just like in the Bible," he said smiling. "I heard you singing when I was in my office and I had to come out just to see what face belonged to that voice of Gods'."

"I wouldn't go *that* far, but that would be me."

"No honestly, that was beautiful. Do you attend services here? I know that is a strange question to ask but I have not completely met everyone just yet, that's why I am looking forward to this homecoming."

"It's ok to ask and no I don't attend here at the present time."

"Are you at any church at the moment?"

"Well, I'm working on that," Rebeccah slowly responded thinking how she was not ready to explain to everyone, especially a Preacher, why she didn't attend churches. She felt she shouldn't have to lie in the house of the Lord and didn't know what to come up with real quick to make it sound like she was not a heathen.

"Well praise God that you made it here today," Brian said pleased that he could possibly get her to attend.

"That's right, Pastor," Terrance interrupted. "She will be here performing at the revival."

"Amen to that, sister," Brian said thinking how her smile made him smile and her pretty hazel eyes that did not look like cheap Swapmeet contacts. He noticed that she had a pretty firm grip and that she didn't feel awkward with him holding her hand for so long. Brian thought it would be better to let her hand go, but she seemed comfortable standing next to him. He was unsure if he was feeling love for her seeing how she literally had taken his breath away. He felt like a man who had been comforted from all of his pains and sorrows. He even felt as if he had been forgiven for all the wrong he had done in his past with her by his side.

"Reebie," Terrance said. "The Pastor and I need to talk for a minute if that's fine with you."

For a minute she thought that what her friend had said was awkward. As if he was asking for her permission. She finally realized that she and Brian had still been holding hands. She let go of his hand and said, "It was nice meeting you Mr., I mean Pastor. Oh heck, oops sorry God, I mean Brian."

"No problem, sister. No problem. See you this Sunday."

Brian glanced at her while she walked away. He needed to know more about this mysterious Rebeccah Carpenter who literally touched him. He hoped he wasn't too obvious in being completely smitten by her.

"So what do you think?" asked Kathy.

"I loved it," Rebeccah excitedly replied. "I have not felt that wonderful in such a long time."

"It's called the Holy Spirit," Kathy reminded her.

"Well whatever you call it, I felt good," she said pleased. "I still do."

"That's good to hear. You *will* be back, right?"

"That I will," Rebeccah said determined to return

again for some more uplifting feelings.

"So what else did you think?"

"About?" she asked unaware of what her friend was referring.

"You know what I mean. Stop playing!"

"Uhm, no I don't really. What do I think about the church?"

"Not even that. What do you think about the Preacher?"

"I didn't think anything about him, Kathy."

"You could have fooled me. I saw how you two were holding each others hands."

"What do you mean? We were praying."

"I mean after prayer. You two would not let go of each other."

"Whatevah, Kat!"

"Say you two, hold up," Terry said while walking up to his friends. "So what do you think?"

"She likes him."

"What! I don't think he meant that, Kat."

"Yes I did."

"Man you two will never stop will you?"

"Come on. You know you checked him out. If I know you as well as I do, you checked him out."

"No I did not," Rebeccah replied while apologizing to the Lord for lying on church ground.

She knew that she did size the man up; just a little. She noticed that he seemed very attractive and he had a nice firm grip of her hand. She had seen that he was very sure of himself and was not at all afraid to meet a stranger. Rebeccah could not take the time to even think of herself being with a man. Her life was much too hectic for someone of his caliber. Besides, her dating a Preacher would definitely be the wrong thing. He would revert back to his old ways if she and he would be together. She never did trust Preachers one bit, and he definitely looked like he had a tainted past that was full of dealing drugs, partying, and even pimping.

"Really Reebie, what do you think?"

"I told you two already, *that* that is not my style. Besides, he is not someone I want or need in my life."

"Oh here we go," replied Terry, "the bitter sister club again."

"No that aint it," Rebeccah interjected. "Ya'll already know how I feel about preachers. All of them have a past. It just aint caught up with them yet."

"All of us have a past, too. But love is love," said Kathy.

"Did you just say love? Nowhere am I even thinking of loving a man right now."

"Whatever!"

"You two brought me here to sing, and that is what I plan to do. Just sing. Nothing more, nothing less. When this revival thing-a-ma-bob is over, I plan on leaving right along with it."

"She did sang though didn't she," said Kathy.

"Of course I did," Rebeccah said being a little cocky.

"But again, girl," Terry reminded her, "it was all because of the Lord."

"Yeah," she said, "and you two little worry warts taking over my schedule helped a little."

"Children, children," interjected Kathy. "Calm down. Who is down for some lunch?"

"I am a little hungry," Terry said grabbing his stomach.

"I need to make a stop first. Whose car are we riding in?"

"It doesn't matter to me."

"I drove the last time," Kathy reminded them both.

"Well, I aint leaving mines here," Rebeccah said looking around the almost empty parking lot.

"Girl, you know you want to leave yours here just so you can run into *Brian* again."

"*Whatever* you think, but I'll follow you two."

Brian sat at his desk in the study still happy from meeting Ms. Carpenter. He thought about how she had really caught his attention. He could not be too obvious though because that was not the image he wanted to put out yet to the congregation; that he was actually looking for Mrs. Right. He wondered if anyone knew much about her personal life besides Brother Hunt. This was the time when he really needed his boy Mike. Mike was good at finding out street information about people for him. She didn't appear to be street at all. She had a certain class about her. He just didn't know what it was. He felt he had seen Rebeccah somewhere before but he could not put his hands on it. He did feel in his heart that she was familiar. From her voice, smile, looks, demeanor, she was a woman that he once knew, but where he couldn't say. Brian sat back and pondered a little more. The more he thought, the more he felt an overwhelming power of love that settled him. He picked up the phone to call his old friend to find out some more information about this mystery woman.

"Ayo, Mike!"

"What's up, brah?"

"I need you to hook me up with something, man."

"Oh, now you coming around. You want a sack?"

"Nah man nah. Not that."

"Oh so now Preacher man needs his homeboy to hook him up?"

"Man it aint like that either," Brian said beginning to be frustrated with his friend.

"So now you saying you too good for me to hook you up with something?"

"Nah man, nah. Will you just stop for a second and listen. Can you help me out or what?"

"Yeah man I can hook you up. What you need, man?"

"I need to know some information on someone."

"Who is he? Is it one of those ugh, what you call them, deacons messin' with you?"

"Nah man, nah!"

"You sure you don't need a sack, man?"

"Man, let me get it out would you?"

"Fa sho then, man. Hurry up tho' I got things to do."

"It's this lady."

"Oh, and you aint hook me up with her, man."

"Nah man, this one is special."

"What kind of special is that?"

"Someone who I need you to find some information on, man."

"Oh word! Man it's like that?"

"Man, if you only knew."

"So what's honey's name?"

"Rebeccah Elise Carpenter, she owns a…"

"You mean the honey that owns the record label?"

"You know her?"

"Man we got a few homies trying to get the hook up at her label. Besides that, she was in this month's issue of SouthSyde Magazine."

"Hhm, SouthSyde Magazine, huh?"

"Yep'per. Say man, what else you need 'cause I got things to do?"

"Just find out what you can for me."

"Fa sho. You know you owe me one, Brain."

"I got you man. I got you."

"Peace, amen, or whatever it is you guys say."

"Man bye," Brian said. He was excited that she was in SouthSyde Magazine.

"Hhm I think I got a copy at the house," Brian found himself thinking out loud. "I know I have seen her somewhere before, but it wasn't in print. I know her from somewhere else. I just feel it in my spirit that I know her from somewhere."

———————

It had taken Brian a minute to get home because Lesha had hemmed him up at the church once again. She had asked him something about herself, as usual ,to bring attention to Brian about how she wanted him. He didn't really contemplate on the conversation because it really didn't matter to him. The only thing he had on his mind was Rebeccah Carpenter, she soothed him. He was thinking about if he had a current issue of SouthSyde Magazine or not at home. Just in case if he didn't, he stopped at the store to purchase one. There she was, the woman that had taken his breath away, right on the cover. She was a fine caramel sister who was very shapely. *"Excuse me Lord, for thinking of her beauty,"* he said out loud. Rebeccah had a beautiful smile which killed him when she smiled at him in the church. He could still hear her singing. It felt like heaven to him, or at least what he thought angels in heaven would sound like.

The story read that she was thirty-three, not much younger than he, which meant that they could connect on the same level. It went on to say that she didn't have any children nor was she married. That was one of the things Brian really wanted to know because he didn't see a ring on her finger. He noticed that most women didn't wear them all the time, which was a shame. *There must be some kind of problem with her,* he thought, especially since she was thirty-three years of age and not married. He realized that he was not married either, but for a woman as gorgeous and together as she was, there had to have been some sort of problem with her. The women in Brian's past did not equal to the lifestyle that he had planned for his future. They were not preacher wife material.

He read the article a little more and found out that she traveled around the world looking for new artist. She loved Jazz and spoken word. She was a writer in her spare time, but most of all she was an artist. The woman was bad as bad could be. Rebeccah was a musician, singer, producer, and a successful entrepreneur. She was a woman after Brian's own heart. He knew she was different than most. Very business oriented, smart, intelligent, and sexy, *"excuse me again father"* he said out loud looking up.

"The main problem is you are single," he said looking at her picture. "Why is a woman of your importance still single, Miss Lady? How come a man has not swept you off your feet yet? Why are you coming around now?

Brian surmised that she may have been a bit bossy for some of the brothers that came into her life and they didn't know how to handle a woman like her. She had no idea whose life she had just walked into. He knew her. The information that he gathered helped him out a bit, but he still needed to know more. He couldn't let her know what he was trying to do, but he wanted to get close to her. He had to plan it out really well. Brian had to make it a situation where she wanted to pursue him. He still had a reputation to uphold as being a preacher. Pursing her would be out of the question.

"Maybe I have seen her on one of my trips with Mike," he said to himself. "Nah she doesn't seem like the type that would go that far by herself. I don't know but one thing I will say is, you are now someone I want to know Ms. Rebeccah Elise Carpenter."

Chapter

4

"Why Rebeccah Elise Carpenter, you look dashing today," Terry said while she had gotten into his car.

"Why thank you, Terry. Is the hat too much?"

"No darling, you look like you have been going to church for years."

She knew she looked good, but she did feel like she had overdone it a little with the wide brim hat she had on. When she went shopping the night before, the sales lady told her that that type of hat set the entire suit off. Rebeccah fell for it and bought it. It had been a long time since she had been to church and nothing in her closet screamed appropriate to wear. She had to go shopping for something because everything she had was either a power suite or club gear. She needed something that would holler she was a continuous church go'er. Rebeccah even purchased a new Bible that had four different translations. Not that she would be reading it that often, but she had to front like she was a woman of God and not a back slider. She even got home and highlighted a few verses that she remembered as a child. Rebeccah knew it was a sin before the 'Living Lord,' but she had to be on her p's and q's after her friends mentioned the Preacher to her. Rebeccah's friends had her thinking about him. She felt deep down that she was not preacher wife material one bit. She did too much of the wrong things in her line of work that would not be conducive of that of a preachers wife at all. Dare she say it? She was completely worldly.

"He was a *little* attractive," she said in the back of her mind but thought she was fooling herself. From his firm grip to that smile that was handsome. His smile, to her, said so much about him. Rebeccah learned to read people a long time ago, especially with the multi-million dollar contracts she dealt with on a daily basis. She had to know who she was dealing with at all times, and body language was what allowed her to make conscious decisions. She could tell that he was a ladies man and at one point in time, he could have been a hustler of some sort. For any man to get up in front of hundreds of people at a time and have them listen to everything that he said, had to have been some sort of hustler in his past. On top of that, she felt he could also be a playboy. *"He had gotten to be some sort of playboy,"* she repeated to herself in her mind. *"Especially by the way that one lady was standing there staring at them the entire time. She seemed very jealous that he was not paying her that much attention and holding my hand. Mr. Playboy indeed."*

"Reebie you okay, girl?" Terry asked.

"Huh? Yeah. Why you ask?"

"You are just quite over there in your seat."

"No, I'm fine. I just have a lot on my mind with this new artist I am signing."

"You want to talk about it?"

"No, I'm ok."

"Who is this in your car?" Dang girl you look *nice.*"

"Thanks Kat, so do you."

"I know, huh?"

"There goes Ms. Vanity as usual," Terry said.

"I know right," Rebeccah agreed.

"Well Terry, let me tell you what happened when I got home last night."

Rebeccah was pleased to know that it was less time for her to listen to her friend Kathy tell an outlandish story, especially since she didn't include Rebeccah's name when announcing her excitement. Besides, she had something else on her mind.

"Now where was I," she said under her breath making sure that they did not hear her. "Oh yeah, that's right stereotypical preachers, players, pimps."

She wondered how many women Brian talked to or went with from the church in general. Rebeccah could spot them right off, when she could see a man and woman's interaction together. The woman always gives it away by their reaction. The men however, are very standoffish, distant. She felt it was down right cold how a brother could sometimes not treat a woman with respect in public, especially if they are seeing each other in private. That was one of the reasons why Rebeccah was single. She didn't want to allow a man to run over her nor treat her like she meant nothing to him in public; or in private. She refused to be played by anyone else again. It happened to her once or maybe twice, but now she had her guard up one hundred percent of the time. She thought that something about this man had caught her attention though. She couldn't place a finger on it, but whatever energy he had, he was good at it.

"She been like this all morning," Terry said. "Rebeccah."

"Huh?"

"Girl, where are you at right now?" Kathy asked chuckling at her friend who was lost in space.

"Oh, I just have a lot on my mind."

"We know," they both said together then laughed. "Shut up!"

"Are you ready for the service?" asked Kathy.

"Of course I am!"

"She is dressed for the part if anything."

Rebeccah knew that they would think that about her, in fact that's what she wanted 'to look the part.' She hoped everyone would think the same at the church, especially the preacher man.

"Service was lovely today, Pastor," Lesha said to Brian who was standing at the sanctuary door.

"Thank you," he said noticing Rebeccah walking by. "Sister Carpenter, it is so good to see you again."

"Why thank you," Rebeccah said.

"I was hoping you would get up and do a solo for us today."

"I wasn't really prepared for that."

"I understand. I hope to see you again back at service this Wednesday for Bible Study."

"You know I am actually kind of busy this week."

"You are never too busy for the Lord."

"I guess you are right," she said smiling a little timidly.

"Oh," Lesha said pushing Rebeccah out of the way. "I'm sorry but Pastor Foster, I wanted to tell you something."

"Well hello again, Sister Walker," he said looking a little upset by Lesha's rudeness.

"I'm so sure," Lesha said looking Rebeccah up and down. "You know I really enjoyed your sermon today. I think that you were actually personally speaking to me. It really felt like it. Especially when you were looking directly at me."

Brian wondered why Lesha was standing in front of him messing up his opportunity to speak with Rebeccah. Brian saw that Rebeccah was beginning to walk away because of Lesha. He wasn't finished with his plan of getting to know her more and wanted her to stay a little longer. He asked the Lord to forgive him for being rude to Lesha but she had really gotten on his last nerves. His opportunity for love was about to walk out of his life and he couldn't let that happen. He already knew what Lesha wanted and it had nothing to do with his sermon, nor church. Nothing at all that dealt with faith, at least not church faith. Did she not get that he was not into her one bit.

He could see that she was trying to block his play and had enough of the silly little game. Ms. Carpenter seriously had his eye and she even looked lovely to him. "*Well minus the hat,*" he thought. "*She could have come without that.*" Other than that, she was a dream that was standing before him until she walked away. He wanted to find a way to talk to her one on one. He had to think quickly on his feet to get her number. Next to him in the foyer on the table was a visitor's card. He picked it up, looked her way, and then called her name.

"Excuse me for a minute, Sister Walker," he said walking past Lesha. "Ms. Carpenter, before you leave I need to ask you something."

As her friends turned around and noticed who was trying to get her attention, one of them said, "Girl, you better go back over there."

"Shut up, Kathy," Rebeccah said nudging her friend before Brian was in ear's reach. She felt a little awkward because she was not sure if Lesha was his woman or not and she didn't want to cause any drama. "Oh I'm sorry, Pastor Foster. I figured you were busy," she said glancing at Lesha who was well on her way to the huddle that was now standing by the visitors table.

"Oh no. That wasn't anything that important," he said while brushing off the idea that anyone would think that he and Lesha had some sort of thing going on.

By then Lesha was standing right behind him acting as if she were fixing something on the visitor's table. He could feel that she was near because everyone glanced her way for a short second as if they had been caught doing something suspicious and then turned their attention back to Brian.

"I wanted to know if you filled out one of our visitor's cards?" he asked.

"No I sure didn't," Rebeccah replied.

"You really need to fill one out. Let me get one for you real quick. You know, we like to keep in touch with our guests whenever they come through." He reached over to the table and picked up a visitors form a little annoyed of the fact that Lesha was there in the way once again. He figured as long as she didn't butt in again, everything would be fine and he could get to finally have a reason to talk to the lady who had intrigued him.

"Not a problem then. I don't mind filling anything out," Rebeccah said as she looked in her new purse that matched her dress and shoes for a pen. *Silly me* she thought; any other time she would be loaded down with pens and this time she could not ask Candice or her friends for help. They were too busy eyeing the fact that she finally had someone who was willing to talk to her without her cursing him out in the process. They were no help at all for her. She looked at Brian and asked, "Do you have a pen?"

"Sure let me..." he said reaching in his jacket for a pen.

"Here you go, Brian," Lesha said reaching around him to hand the pen to Rebeccah.

"Why thank you, Sister Walker," he replied a little annoyed and hoped it didn't show on his face. "Rebeccah make sure you put all of you information on there. Ok when....." he began to ask and noticed that Lesha was now standing next to him, "....when would be a good time for one of the deacons to call you?"

"Well, I'll put my office number down just in case they need to call during the day. To answer your question anytime in the morning is fine."

"Will do," he said as he took the visitors card smiling.

"I'll take that for you, Brian, and give it to one of the deacons if you don't mind," Lesha demanded while reaching out for the visitor's card.

"No that's okay, Sister Walker," he snatched his hand back and wished that she would go somewhere to leave him alone. She could see that he was a little angry but didn't care one bit because she decided to stay around for the outcome.

"I got it, thank you," he said. He wanted to know why she had still been around messing up his game that he was working on. He really wanted to know more about Rebeccah. He wished Lesha would go far-far away to another country, but he knew that would not happen. "*Sorry Lord*," he mumbled because he knew his thoughts were in the wrong.

"I'll see you all later. I don't want to interrupt your conversation," Rebeccah said looking at Lesha and then Brian.

"Thank you," Lesha said eyeing her up and down. "At least *she* knows I'm talking to you."

"Sister Walker," Brian said to her as if scolding her.

"Well, she *was* being rude," Lesha childishly replied while pointing at Rebeccah.

"I'm sorry about that," he said.

"No problem. No problem at all. You two have a blessed day," Rebeccah said.

"You do the same," he said wanting to say more to her and to apologize but she started walking away.

"Hhmph! Now as I was saying, Brian, you have really touched me today and I thank you so much for your generosity towards me."

Brian had found himself wishing again that Lesha would leave him alone and that she would get her arm off from around his waist. He wondered how come all women could not be classy like Rebeccah. Her smile and hazel eyes had gotten him. The card she filled out was so that he could call her, which he would definitely do. He planned not to call her right away; he didn't want to seem anxious. One thing he knew for sure was that she would definitely be hearing from him, and not one of the deacons.

"Did you see how that girl just got in the way?"

"I wouldn't pay her any attention. She's a hater."

"Always has been and always will be."

"Is he her man or something?"

"Who, the Pastor? Nah!"

"Why are you two laughing?"

"Because I don't think anyone in their right mind would even touch her with a ten-foot pole."

"Yeah, right! Even if I was interested in woman, I wouldn't even think about touching her."

"What? Why you guys say that?"

"*Because*, the scoop is she is a tramp from ways back."

"That's right. A straight jezebel!"

"Ya'll mean a hoe, right?"

"You said it, sister."

"She would turn that mans world around if he ever messed with her."

"And you know how straight legged he is."

"Kind of *too* straight if you ask me."

"I always swore up and down that he was gay."

"I could have picked that out a long time ago hon, and gay he is not."

"Why are you guys busy talking about the man so?"

"*Because* girl, that's what we do. You should know that!"

"Well you know I heard he used to be a drug dealer."

"A what! See that's why I don't go to church anymore."

"That aint the half of it, girl…"

"What do you mean?"

"Girl, don't let him fool you. C'mon, a single man that is around our age. He could have been doing anything before now, or ever!"

"Something like what?"

"Anything!"

"Everything!"

"So why are you two so excited in tryin' to hook me up with a pimp, dealer, or whatever?"

They began to laugh again.

"Why are you two laughing?"

"Girl, we just playing."

"We just wanted to see if you were interested in him or not."

"Yeah, you should have seen the look on your face just then."

"Ya'll play too much for me. *Way* too much," Rebeccah said beginning to realize that maybe she was a little concerned and that she should not keep her hopes up.

"He is straight legged though. We checked him out a long time ago when he gave us his resume'."

"Oh *sure*."

"Girl, don't be that way. You should have seen how he was really into you."

"What do you mean into me?"

"I mean he was rushing to give you a card to fill out and everything."

"Well," Terry interrupted, "he would have had her there longer except Lesha was right there in her and his face hating on the poor child."

"All I know is," Rebeccah interjected, "you two still play too much for me."

"Whatever, girl!"

They started chuckling again and talking about an

entirely new topic. They really had her head going in circles. She was glad Terry and Kathy had another church to go to because she was not in the mood for traveling anywhere else with them. She just wanted to go home and think about how wonderful her day had been. She had been to church in God knows how long and she actually had learned a thing or two. One thing she learned was not to wear any more hats, even if she thought they were cute. The second thing she learned was she needed a smaller Bible because the one she had was way too heavy to carry.

She made it home, walked in her condo and sat down on her plush sofa. As she sat there, she wondered why Brian was rushing to get her info. When she shook his hand she noticed they were callused which meant he did some hard work. They didn't look like hands of a man who dealt drugs, or pimped. A drug dealers hands are nicely clean and manicured without calluses. Nope those were definitely hands of a man who did some hard work.

Her friends were right in saying that a single man their age was unusual. What was in his past? She couldn't put her finger on it. He was definitely able to move the crowd at church when he preached. He even had her moving back in forth in her seat while he was preaching. He seemed very sure of himself, almost a little cocky but that made him even more interesting and cute. What was strange to her was the subject he preached on was something that she had been troubled with all week. He had preached about making life changes.

Rebeccah had major changes she was dealing with. She wondered how he knew that. He could have been talking to several other people besides her. It was strange though that he addressed the very questions she had written down in her journal. She wondered if Terry had something to do with it. If he had spoken to the preacher beforehand and told him what she'd been going through. Her personal life was the lessons topic for the morning when she really sat down and thought about it. He was speaking as if no one else was there in the church except for him and her. She figured that was his male magnetism or that power that preachers can have sometimes when they speak in public.

Rebeccah thought again about how her friends should have not told her about a past, even if they were playing around. Regardless of what it was, that would stick in the back of her mind for a long time, especially when she would see him again. Again, she contemplated on how he knew so much about her life and how he was able to read her up and down. She needed to speak to Terry later that evening. Brian Foster had hit to close to home for her and Terry could answer her questions. She figured she needed to go to church on Wednesday night just to see what he would have to say again or if he had gotten his information about her from one of her friends.

While Brian sat down at his desk, he hoped that he didn't scare Rebeccah away. What he really hoped was that Lesha hadn't scared her away. She was completely and unacceptably rude. She had almost messed up his entire game plan, but at least he was able to get her office number. He wanted her home number, but for now what he had gotten would suffice. He hadn't heard from his boy Mike. He knew that Mike had been slipping lately. He didn't know if he should check up on him or not. He could have possibly had a new lady friend that kept him occupied. Mike was entirely late in getting Brian more information so he had to step up his game in order to get next to Rebeccah. He thought what would be better than to go directly to the source anyway. She told him that it would be ok to call her at work so he thought he might as well do just that. He wasn't sure what to say to her. Of course he did need to know information about her for the church. Normally the deacon's at church would do the calling and they knew exactly how to approach a new member or visitor. Brian knew she was more to him than just a visitor. She was someone that he could see himself being with for a long time to come. He had to think of something quick in order to make the conversation worth her while. After all, she was a busy woman. Luckily for Brian, he worked fast on his feet and could make up things on the spot. He felt that he was blessed with being able to work quick. He picked up the phone and dialed the number.

"Melodic Voices, this is Candice speaking. How may I help you?"

"Yes Candice, hi this is Pastor Brian Foster from The Holy Tabernacle of God. May I speak to Ms. Rebeccah Carpenter?"

"Sure, please hold." For a second Candice was unaware of who was calling. It didn't dawn on her until she had gotten Rebeccah on the line that the call came from *her* Pastor.

"Rebeccah, you have a call on line one. It's Pastor Foster."

"Pastor Foster? Who? Oh. Ok send it through."

Rebeccah was shocked that she would hear from Brian so soon. She thought that he was still hemmed up by the lady from the church. She kind of smiled for a second realizing that he was taking the first step in getting to know her. It also meant that she would be able to ask him how he knew so much about her when he preached in church the past Sunday.

"Melodic voices, this is Rebeccah. How may I help you?"

"Hello, sister," he said gleefully. "This is Brian."

"Hello, Brian. How are you today?"

"Just fine. Just fine." Now that Brian was on the phone with her he had gotten a little nervous. This had never happened before. He had to brace himself again just to keep his mind straight on the prize.

"I hope I didn't disturb you."

"No, you're ok. I needed a break anyway. How may I help you today, its not Terry is it?"

"Oh no, not at all. I was just doing my routine calls."

"Routine calls? What is it," here we go she thought. "Was it something that I have done or didn't do?"

"No, no not that either. It's just you were a guest and we normally do a mandatory call and touch bases with our guest."

"Ok touch on then. Oops sorry. I guess that was the wrong thing to say wasn't it?"

"It's ok. No need to apologize. We all slip up sometimes," he said smiling and then caught his composure again. "Well, what I wanted to know was if you were a member of any particular church?"

"Who put you up to this call, was it Terry or Kathy?"

"Put me up to it? No, it is just routine."

"I'm sorry. This just bothers me sometimes just because I haven't been going to church at one particular place doesn't mean that I do not believe in God."

"No one has said that, sweetie," Brian said and then figured that this call was not going exactly the way he planned it would at all. He thought he may have called her at the wrong time but continued to press forward. "You seem like a very intelligent woman and a few people have been telling me some things about you. I felt it is better to go to the source than to make any assumptions…"

"Telling you what about me?" she interrupted.

"Well that part isn't that important..."

"And who has been telling you things?" she snapped.

"Oh it is not any of your friends. Some of the deacons at the church weren't sure where you were in your faith and they didn't know if it would be right for you to sing during revival, especially if you are not affiliated with any churches around here."

"See here we go. This is why I stopped going to church to begin with. Everyone is always in my business with these so-called rules they make up and if they don't know me they will make up things about me. Why is it so hard for folks to just accept you for who you are? I mean it does say come, as you are, right? Why is it like my grandmother always used to tell me, you find more Christians out of the church than you do in the church? Why is it so important for someone to know who I am affiliated with? Isn't it just good that I came to sing for God? You gotta start somewhere. I mean you really have to excuse me on this but, this just ticks me off to no end."

Brian sat there thinking that he may have just made her upset. He needed to control the conversation real quick because he didn't want to make her any more upset. "No it's not that, sweetie. It's just we need to make sure that you do believe in God and what faith you have in order to appease our members." *Lord, please forgive me for thinking on my toes right now because I think I have really made Ms. Lady mad. I didn't know that this was a touchy subject for her.* "I do apologize for upsetting you. I am just doing my duties."

"Well I understand that you are working and all for the Lord, but at this moment it just really burns me up that people pry into my business. I mean, I do not have anything against you at all. I just don't like being forced to answer any unnecessary questions."

"I understand that completely. I would like to set up a

meeting to talk with you a little more if you don't mind. I mean it will be a little more in-depth than now."

"In depth! What more do you need to know aside that I do not belong to any particular church? You know, let's just make this a little easier for the both of us. If there is going to be a problem with my singing at the church for the revival, than what do I need to do to make this a little easier for everyone because right now I have gotten a little upset."

Brian asked himself why he had taken the approach that he did. He needed to polish up on his game with her. She was not the average woman. He could kind of understand because she was a businesswoman of a major label, which means she did not take any nonsense from anyone. He didn't want to be placed in the category with just *anyone* though. "I am so sorry, Rebeccah. I did not mean to offend you in any way. However, the best thing to do is, since I know that you do believe in God, is to repent, confess, and then be baptized."

"Uhm, excuse me, I have already been baptized."

He knew she was really upset because she became very short with him. What could he do? He figured she was very bossy, why else would a woman like that be single. She threw a curve ball at him and he was not expecting it at all. The woman on the phone was not the same woman that he heard singing on Saturday, nor the woman he saw smiling at him the day before; timid.

"Hello?"

"I'm still here. Sorry someone just walked in. The only other thing that I suggest is that you transfer your membership with us."

"And how do I do that?"

"By letter or in front of the church."

"You know what," Rebeccah caught herself before going off. "Uhm, never mind. Ok, is there anything else that I need to do, I have an appointment coming in."

"No actually that should be it, but I would like to set up a meeting with you as soon as I can."

"Ok sure uhm, I have a call coming in but thank you for being concerned."

"Not a problem and again I do apologize for offending you in any way."

"No problem at all."

"God bless."

"Uhm, ahuh."

"Bye." He knew that he had messed up entirely. He finally saw how feisty of a lady she was. He knew that the conversation did not work out as planned. Brian wondered where he went wrong. He knew that from then on out he would have to start recognizing that she was not one of those sisters that he could just call on a whim. His charm did not work with her at all. Instead of bringing her closer to wanting him, he sent her three steps away. He knew that it would take a lot of work to make her want to be a part of his life. *Lord, what do I need to do?*

Rebeccah thought that there went another man in her life who had pissed her off. She couldn't figure out why people could not stay out of her business and just let her be. Church, to her, was just church and the entire thing on judging her seemed to go against what she remembered from Bible study as a child. She didn't know why she should have to change her lifestyle just to sing one Sunday in church. The idea to her was obnoxious.

"Another man who has pissed me off! Ugh!"

She loved who she was, what she became, and she loved God. If it wasn't for His love for her, she would not have the things that she had. She was thankful for all that she had, and knew God was a part of it. She felt she didn't do anything in her life wrong in her eyes. She tithed, at least when she could. She honored her father and mother, even though they were thousands of miles away. Rebeccah wondered what had gotten her so upset with Brian. She knew that she could not be upset with herself. She also knew that she did not need to change. Everything was just fine the way it was for her. She may have been a little harsh on the poor guy. The entire conversation had made her upset again; upset to the point that she changed her mind about how cute she thought he was. He wanted her to alter her life just so she could sing. *Get over it.* She needed to really speak to Terry but it would have to wait.

"Candice. Send in my first appointment, please."

"Yes, ma'am."

"Terrance Tramain Hunt, why did you sick that man on me yesterday?"

"What do you mean sick that man on you?"

"You sent *that man* my way, didn't you?"

"What are you rambling on about, Reebie?"

"That man had the nerve to say that I needed to become a member of the church if I decided to sing in the choir."

"And what is wrong with that?"

"What is wrong? What is wrong is I don't want anyone telling me how I need to lead my life just so I can sing. I can do all of this without having to be a member of a church!"

"Reebie, you are taking this too far."

"No I am not, Terrance *Tramain* Hunt!"

"Yes you are, Rebeccah *Elise* Carpenter. What exactly

did he say to you?"

"He told me that in order for me to sing and to keep the peace in the church, I needed to become a member and at the rate I feel right now, they could all just kiss my..."

"Reebie hold on, girl. Don't get your panties all in a bunch. You have to look at it from his perspective. The reason why he did that was because he may have been pressured by some of the deacons. They may have questioned him about his job. If he doesn't see what happens in the church and check on visitors, he could lose his position. You know being a pastor of a church doesn't just mean getting in a pulpit and shouting. It's an actual job believe it or not."

"Whatever!"

"Whatever some nothing. If you had a potential employee walking around your office building for a couple of days and doing office work like they belonged there without you hiring them, what would you do?"

"I'd.."

"Yeah, you'd question everybody there why that person was walking around your office and you would also approach *said* phony employee. Am I right or wrong?"

"Okay, okay you are right. But still, I didn't like the way he came at me."

"See you are trippin', Reebie. He may have also been interested in you but if I know you, you probably pushed him back all the way to Africa."

"Shut up, Terrance. I did not."

"You know you did."

"Nope."

"Yes you did, girl."

"Okay maybe not as far as Africa, but I was a little rude."

"*Well*, now you need to apologize to him."

"Now you and I both know it is hard for me to do that."

"Well make it un-hard. Besides, you can't be making me look bad, girl. I need you for the revival."

"I ain't going to be a member there, Terry."

"You don't know what the Lord has in store for you. What you need to work on first is apologizing and then the rest will fall into place."

"Man you suck."

"I know tell me something new."

"Oh I can't stand you."

"Yes you can."

"Check this out, honey, I don't mean to cut this short but I have some company coming over. But think about what I just said and apologize to the man."

"How do I do that?"

"Go with your heart. I gotta go. Someone is already at my door."

"Bye, man."

"Cya later, girl."

Rebeccah wondered how in the heck was she suppose to apologize to the preacher man. This was all new to her. She wondered if sending flowers would work. "Nah that wont work," she said to herself out loud. Then she thought she could treat him to dinner, but then reconsidered because that approach would be too desperate.

"What about shoots, what about?" she said asking herself again while walking around her office. No one had ever made her fidget around so; potential clients, deals, or any other man. Making up to him for being so rude earlier was something she felt in her heart she had to do. He was a nice guy and Terrance could have been right. Maybe he was trying to find a way to get to know her better. She figured she ruined it completely because she was about to curse the man out and she was very short with him on the phone. He was just a messenger doing his job. She didn't want him to lose it because of her and her attitudes.

"Candice, can you come into the office for a minute?"

"Yes ma'am."

"Candice, I am in a dilemma and I need your help."

"Ok, I can do that."

"Tell me about your Preacher."

"Oh you mean, Pastor Foster? He is a good man. He has me teaching the youth at the church."

"Really? I didn't know that you were that active."

"I try. I am also a mentor to a couple of the young girls. He believes in working with the community and helping out as many people as we can. He says I work real well with kids."

"That's good, but what else is it that you know about him besides church stuff?"

"Not much really. I don't see him outside of the church that often, well, except for the church picnic."

"And did you notice anything that he liked?" Rebeccah asked while sitting on her sofa in the office.

"Aside from food, not really."

"I see that you are not much help here," Rebeccah said wondering sometimes why she hired her. At certain points Candice could be a little spacey. She knew how to handle office work, she even would work late right along with Rebeccah, but getting outside information took her some time to respond.

"That will be all then. After you finish your work you can go home early."

"Thanks, Ms. Carpenter. Sorry I wasn't that much help."

"Not a problem and you are welcome."

"Oh! There is a person I can call and ask. My Aunt Suella Belle."

"Aunt Suella Belle? I won't even comment. Ok continue."

"She's Pastors Secretary and she can help me out with

some information. I'll go and call her right now."

"Great, you do that then." Rebeccah sat up on the sofa while she watched Candice walk out of the office like a schoolgirl who did something promising. Rebeccah knew she was good for something.

Chapter
5

"Is there anything else I can do for you, Pastor?" Sister Jenkins asked grinning from ear to ear.

"No, Sister. That will be all for now. Is everything fine?" Brian noticed that she was extra happy.

"Oh sure. Just fine. That it sure is. All fine," she said grinning even harder.

Sometimes she reminded him of his mother. At one point she looked as if she could have been a southern belle. She took care of him as if he was her child by making sure he had a well rounded meal. She would bring him home cooked meals because she knew that he was a bachelor. At times he would even find himself calling her mother. She didn't mind one bit. Since his mother had died several years prior, he was thankful that there was someone around who looked out for his best interest. She had been walking around that afternoon grinning like a Cheshire cat.

It was another Tuesday at the church and Brian could not help but think about how upset he had made Rebeccah on the phone the day before. He had messed it up for any potential chance for them to hook up. He hadn't quite given up hope, but he would wait for her call the next time around. He wanted to set up a meeting with her but he knew being patient was one thing he needed to have in order to work on her schedule. It was now five o'clock and he had completed his lesson that he was going to teach for Wednesday night Bible Study. He finished all of his calls, signed a few checks and it was now time for him to step out of the office and head home. He was going to call Mike to see what he was getting into but felt he should concentrate on other things; one being Ms. Rebeccah Carpenter. He wondered how to right something that he wronged with her. She was a bit feisty for his taste, but that only meant that she was very strong. He liked a strong willed woman. She needed to be taught a few things about dealing with him. He was not one of her employee's and he wanted her to know it. He did need a woman of her caliber in his life who knew what she wanted and who was able to bring him back to reality when he needed it the most; a woman who would have his back one hundred and ten percent.

"Good night, sister," he said while closing his office door. "You and the Deacons are going to lock up, right?"

"Yes sir. We have it under control," she said still grinning from ear to ear. "You have a wonderful evening, Pastor."

"You do the same, Sister Jenkins."

As Brian walked out of the back door, he saw a stretched limo between him and his car. A tall brother was standing at the back door.

"The lady is waiting for you, sir." as he opened the door for Brian to get in.

"Lady! For who? Me?"

"Yes sir, for you."

He moved closer to the limo hoping that he wouldn't find Lesha sitting in the back scantily clothed. Thank God however, that he knew that she had went out of town on family business. He peeped in and low and behold there was the woman who was completely on his mind all day. It finally dawned on him why Mama Jenkins was grinning.

"Ms. Carpenter," he said a little astonished. "It is nice

to see you."

"You too, Brian. So, are you going to stand out there or come in?"

He noticed again how beautiful she was. She had on an oriental dress with her hair pinned up. She seemed very Asian and he liked the entire look, he could not say anything wrong about the woman one bit. She was very together. He was reluctant at first to step in but she gave him a look that made him realize that she would not act the same way she did on the phone a few days prior.

"I guess I better get in, huh? Ms. Carpenter. Is everything fine?

"Yeah it's fine," she said with a bright smile that melted his heart.

Brian could not help but admire her beauty.

"Before we go, may I get the keys to your car?"

"Huh? My keys? Oh my keys. Sure, I mean. Uhm, what exactly do you need them for?"

"Trust me," she said holding out her hand waiting for his keys and then looked into his eyes. "Can you trust me?"

"Yes I can trust you," Brian said thinking that this was not the same woman that was short with him on the phone. The woman sitting next to him left him speechless and he knew in his heart that he could trust her.

"Where are we going," he asked trying to break his nervousness.

"Can you keep a secret?" she asked him again while looking directly into his eyes.

"A secret," he really thought she was beautiful and by her looking directly at him made him even more nervous. "Yes, I can keep a secret."

"Good. So can I," she grinned seriously.

She had to laugh at her answer, which made him laugh a little, too. He could not get over the fact of her beauty and how calm she was. She did not seem as nervous as him which he tried covering up.

"I am having my driver drop your car off at your condo."

"Condo? How does your driver know where I live? I am not insured for another driver or...."

"Don't worry about it. Everything is taken care of and he knows where to drop it off."

"So you have it like this, huh?"

"You can say yes that I do."

"Really, Sister Carpenter?"

"You know my real name is Rebeccah. My friends call me Reebie."

"Ok Reebie. I mean Rebeccah. What exactly is going on here?"

"I take it you were not to fond of surprises as a child?"

"No, I liked surprises, but I was a child. Now I am an adult."

"Really? Small world."

"Yes really. Look, are you hijacking me or kidnapping me or something?"

"Not really."

"I have a busy day tomorrow."

"Really?"

"Seriously, what is going on?"

"I can drop you off right here if you want or if you feel uncomfortable. Driver, pull over."

"Yes ma'am," the driver said from the front.

"No wait, wait. Don't do that," he said not wanting to be left stranded on the side of the road since they were now far from the church. He especially didn't want whatever was about to happen end. He wanted to see what Rebeccah had up her sleeves. When he looked at her, he noticed that she had beautiful dimples when she smiled.

"You want to keep going then?"

"Yeah, sure."

"Keep going, driver."

"Yes ma'am," he said pulling back into traffic.

"You have a beautiful smile," Brian said.

"Why thank you. Yours isn't so bad either."

She seemed really nice to him, he just wished he knew what to say to her and how to say it. It was really one of his most awkward moments.

"I hope you aren't afraid of heights?"

"Me, nah not really."

"Good, because we are at the airport now."

"Airport! What in Gods creation do you have me doin'?"

She gave him a stern look as if to say if he did not follow through with her program, she would leave him right at the tarmac.

"Ok. Ok, missy. I'm following. I do have one question though?"

"Sure what's that?"

"Do you do this with everyone, because I think I would be afraid of you, especially if I didn't know that you sound like an angel when you sing?"

"I wouldn't say that I do this with everyone. Right now it's just you," she said glancing out of the limousine window then looking back at Brian. "And thank you for the compliment. I don't think I have heard someone compare me to an angel before."

"You did, do. And you are welcome."

Rebeccah had gotten out of the limo and Brian followed behind her. He realized that he wasn't as dressed up as she was.

"I feel like I am a little underdressed for where we are going. Wherever that may be."

"No not at all. You are just fine. Matter of fact, we have a bag already packed for you. If you want to change into some jeans, you can."

"Jeans! What jeans? Wait a minute, wait a minute more importantly, how did you get a bag already packed for me?"

"Just like you Brian, I have friends in high places," she said chuckling at the joke she just made.

"I can see this," he said as they walked into the Jet. "But If I change then what are you going to do?"

"I have luggage already packed, too. I just came from a meeting with a few potential clients in Asia."

"Asia?"

"Yeah. I'm debating on if I should sell the company or not."

"Why would you want to sell? From what I hear, you are doing very well for yourself. And from what I see right now, the columns I read, they do not lie," as he said while looking around the plushed-out jet.

"Yeah well, I do ok. Sometimes I feel I need to change my life. I don't know, but right now at this moment, this isn't about me."

"Then what is it about if it is not about you?"

"Right now it is about fastening your seatbelt," she said as she reached over him to grab the belt from behind the seat. "Buckle up for safety."

Rebeccah looked at Brain smiled, winked, then sat in her leather lounger, and then proceeded to buckle in before take off.

Rebeccah realized that Brian had no clue as to what she had planned for him. Thanks to Candice and her Aunt Suella Bell Jenkins, she was able to plan a quick trip to California. Brian had a secret that was the weirdest thing Rebeccah could ever imagine. She figured she needed to apologize some kind of way to him for her harshness, and she always did things that were unexpected. She was pretty callous to him and from what Candice's aunt said, he needed to take a short break. It was hard for Rebeccah to keep her cool and not tell Brian where they were headed. It took her some thought, but after hearing about Brian's mother passing she knew exactly where to go.

"So is everything okay for you over there?"

"Yes, it's fine," he said clinching his armrest.

"Do you fly?"

"Not a lot."

"I can tell."

"How is that?"

"By the way you are holding on to your seat as if your life depended on it."

"That obvious, huh?"

"Kind of. Don't worry though; we are in good hands with the pilot."

"That's good to know."

"Yeah, especially since he got fired from a major airline for drinking while flying."

"What?"

"Nah, I'm just playin'," she laughed. "I'm just playing. Loosen up a little."

"That wasn't funny. I was praying four times over after that last comment you made."

"I know. Bad timing, right?"

"Just a little," he said.

"Well to ease your mind, I have your bag here. If you would like to change into your jeans and a comfortable shirt that may help you relax a little."

"You think changing clothes will help me relax?"

"Not really, but I thought my company would."

He grinned a little to show that he could at least try to relax.

"Is there somewhere I can change?"

"Yes. The restroom is right behind the last two seats on your left."

"The last two seats?"

"Yes the last two."

"On my left." he said while walking to his right.

She guessed the altitude was getting to him a little because he could not tell his left from his right. She found it a little entertaining to see a man who seemed to have so much control look so lost. "No silly, on your other left."

"Oh, that left. Thanks," he said trying not to look ridiculous even though it was a bit too late. It had taken him about fifteen minutes before he came out of the restroom freshly changed. He looked nice in average clothes she thought. He was very tall, at least taller than her, with a smile that could light up a room. She thought that the man that was standing before her, even though he was a man of the cloth, was very handsome. He was not overweight like most preachers she had seen on television. She wondered why he was not married because any woman in her right mind should have been honored to be with a man like Brian.

"This plane is just like the President of the United States."

"Have you flown with the President before?"

"No, but I have seen pictures of it. Are you wearing the dress that you have on to this undisclosed location that you and I are going to?"

"Now what did I say about asking questions," she said while he looked at her as if he were a little hurt by her response. His entire demeanor changed again. Rebeccah decided to change hers as well. Instead of being on a business level she should treat him like a friend. After all, she was doing all of this because of her attitude.

"I too will be changing. I don't think I would fit in. Standing next to you in some jeans and me all dolled up would not work. It wouldn't feel right. I am going to change here in just a second. Help yourself to something to drink or snack if you'd like. The refrigerator is right behind you and the snacks are in the cabinet above. I'll be right back."

"Ok."

"By the way, do not bother my pilots or ask my assistant for any information. Remember they know that this is a surprise and they may get fired if they speak to you about where we may be headed."

"Yes ma'am. Will do. I think I will just get myself a soda to drink and have a seat right back here. When you get back I will be a good boy and not move."

"Good. Just remember no out of the ordinary questions because I know you have a way of getting things out of people. And no eating too much, we can't spoil the surprise."

"No ma'am not at all. I will be on my best behavior."

She tapped him on his shoulder while she walked away as if to scold a little child in case he would think of doing anything wrong. She hoped that no one would slip up and tell him exactly where they were headed. If she knew her crew as well as she did, they would not do it. But somehow she believed Brian would scare them into telling the truth. They knew that he was a preacher and preachers sometimes had a way with getting what they wanted from people.

Brian looked around and noticed the nice set up. Rebeccah had everything going on for herself. The jet was enormous and laid out to a T. It looked like every seat was covered in brown leather and black granite was around the bar area. Even the appliances were all black or had some form of wood grain. She even dressed like long money. She did not have on a thirty-dollar dress that could have been purchased from the swap meet. Her dress looked original. He wondered what type of meeting she went to and if it was really in Asia. It could have been by the way she looked. From the blue oriental dress to her hair up like an Asian doll, she seemed as if she was working on impressing an emperor of china. When he read the article about her in SouthSyde Magazine, it didn't mention how wealthy she truly was. He wondered why she was spending so much time with him. She seemed like she could be with any man that she wanted, from a billionaire to an athlete. He couldn't help but think again why she was literally flying solo.

"I see you didn't move from your seat."

"No ma'am, I sat here like a good boy."

"Good."

When she stood next to his chair, she took his breath away once again. She had changed into a pair of jeans, T-shirt (not the average t-shirt but long money t-shirt), some sneakers, and her hair was down. Brian realized that he was eyeing her real hard which made her feel a little uncomfortable, so she sat down in her seat.

"What?" Rebeccah asked.

"Huh?"

"Why are you looking at me like I turned into the ugly monster?"

"No, you didn't turn into ugly. You are just even more beautiful. That is if you don't mind my saying so."

"No, I don't mind one bit," she said while pulling her hair back into a ponytail and placing a cap on her head. "You just worried me for a minute because I thought I might have chosen the wrong clothes."

"No you are fine," one hundred percent is what he wanted to say to her. *Lord I can see myself being with this woman for the rest of my life*. It wasn't the money or the jet that caught his attention about her. What did catch his attention was how beautiful she looked, from dress up to jean down. She was a nice caramel toned sister who was heavy but in a good kind of way. No one could say she was like those Hollywood type Barbie dolls that was plastered on every magazine, billboard, or what have you. Rebeccah was a corn fed down south sister who was confident. Brian had seen that she could be pretty mean but overall, that did not bother him one bit. He saw something more in her than just the façade that she put out, something deeper that was loving.

"Why are you staring at me so hard? I thought you weren't *supposed* to stare at a woman or something like that?"

"I am still a man, Rebeccah," when he said her name it sounded sweet to him and it fit her completely. "If I see something that is beautiful, I am definitely going to look. I can't help it. But if it is bothering you, I will stop."

"You're ok, but you have me a little worried is all. I mean, how will the people at church view you if they saw you in this light?"

"I haven't done anything wrong at all. God places things of beauty on this earth for us to enjoy and admire. It's when you lust for or think wrongly about something that He looks down upon you."

"Is *He* looking down upon you now?"

"Oh, I see you have jokes, huh? I am not lusting. I am just admiring your God given beauty."

"Why thank you Brian. You didn't bother my pilots did you?"

"Of course I didn't. Although, I did slide a note under the door to tell him to announce when we get to our location."

"No you didn't!"

"Your right, I didn't. I just wanted to see if you would get mad at me again."

"Nope I'm not going to get mad because like I said earlier, they know not to give out any information what-so-ever unless if I give them the okay to do so."

"So you really have it like that, huh?"

"Yeah I got it like that," she said proud of her accomplishments. "Not to sound cocky or anything like that. This is however, still a business that I run."

"And how big is your business really?"

"Well, I take care of a lot. As you know I have my label, which seems to be doing really good. We have several platinum selling artists, all in hip hop and R&B."

"Do you do Gospel music?"

"Me do Gospel!? I don't think that would be the right thing for me to touch. Especially with some of the artist I have on my label."

"Really. Like who?"

"Million Dolla Maker. MDM for short."

"I've heard of him."

"You have, have you?"

"Yes I have. Again, I am still a man from this world not from a Holy place. Just because I listen to certain music doesn't mean I believe what is being said."

"So then, why do you listen to that *kind* of music?"

"I have to know what kind of person I am dealing with when I need to teach or guide them closer to God."

"Teach or guide. What is wrong with the music that my label puts out? Wait, don't answer that." Rebeccah felt a little ashamed and embarrassed. She began to wonder why she had brought him out so far away from Tennessee to surprise him. He was no one that was familiar to her world. Her world was full of parties, drinking, late night, and after parties. She cringed thinking that she would possibly go to hell for inviting him into her world. The more she thought about it, she realized that the plan could have been the wrong thing to do altogether. She didn't want to bring a good man to the evil side, especially since he was a preacher.

"Reebie, is everything okay?"

"Yeah sure," she said as her stomach began to tighten over the thought of him sitting in the chair across from her on her jet.

"Is it something I said?"

"No, you're fine. I'm just having second thoughts about all of this."

"Second thoughts about what?"

"Maybe it is not good that you should be seen with me."

"And why is that?"

"Because of what I do. I don't want to influence a man of God into doing anything evil."

"You haven't done anything wrong," he said consoling her.

"Are you sure about that? I think I may have deceived you into doing something evil without giving you a chance to make a decision."

"Look, switch the thought around to make it better. Evil reversed means live, which we all must do. I am alive and I am human just like you. You did not force me to do something that I didn't want to do. In fact, my opportunity to speak up was before I even stepped into the limo. Now my second chance was when I gave you my car keys. So there is no way that I did not have a choice in coming with you. I had every opportunity imagined but I want to live, too. I wanted to know what this was all about. It also felt like this was an opportunity for me to apologize for the other day."

"You apologize? You have no need to apologize to me."

"I have every right to apologize. I assumed and approached you in a way that I should not have. I need to be honest with you. When I called you I had other ulterior motives. I didn't want to *just* talk to you to see if you belonged to a church or not. That part is true, but the other reason why I called was to get to know you a little better. Do you honestly think a man of God would have to call every single female visitor that came into the church?"

"I don't know."

"Come on, think about it. That's why there are deacons and a secretary for that. I specifically called you because I wanted to know more about you."

"That's why that one sister was hating on me?"

"Yes, you mean Sister Walker. Yeah. She was right when she said that the deacons could call you, but I wanted to do the talking. I couldn't pass up on someone as beautiful as you are. There is this mystique about you that keeps calling out to me. So I am the one that should apologize for approaching you wrongfully; which means we were both guilty."

Rebeccah sat in silence for a minute thinking about what he had said. She didn't know the he had tried that hard to get to know her. She had a gut feeling that she was still wrong for bringing him so far away from home. *Lord please forgive me if I lead this man in the wrong direction.* She looked up and noticed that he had been looking at her. This time it did not bother her one bit. This time, she felt at ease as if nothing could go wrong and that everything would be ok. She grinned a little at him because the jet started dropping and he held on to his armrest again.

"Ms. Carpenter we are about to land," the pilot announced over the intercom.

"You might want to fasten up again, Brian. The fun is about to begin." He looked at her with a smile and with a look that he didn't want to finish the conversation. He also had a look of what kind of adventure he was about to get into. He couldn't wait for the jet to land.

She didn't want to say another word because she felt she would tell him too much about their excursion they were about to take. She needed to apologize and make a good impression on him, especially now that she knew a little about how he felt towards her.

Brian could not believe that he had just told Rebeccah the truth. In his past he would have never opened up that quick. He needed to apologize to her because he was in the wrong and he couldn't carry that burden on his heart anymore. He was glad to see her a little humble. He could tell that she felt a little ashamed about what she did for a living. He wanted to let her know that everything would be okay but when he was about to, the jet lowered a little and he had gotten a little dizzy. He guessed the Lord didn't want him to share anything else with her. Brian knew that everyone had to go through their own convictions and realize their own faults. He guessed that she had to figure out what her responsibility was before she could move any further with the Lord.

"Why are you grinning so hard?"

"Oh nothing, I was just thanking God for allowing us to land safely."

"You don't like flying?"

"I fly when I have to, but it doesn't mean I like it too well."

"I used to be that way. But since I travel so much now, I get use to it."

"Can I ask you something, Reebie?"

"Sure shoot."

"Where did you say that meeting was that you had with those potential buyers?"

"I didn't say, but if you must know, I was in Japan."

As the jet began slowing down on the runway, Brian thought that Rebeccah was a woman after his own heart. She traveled worldwide, had class, and was beautiful. He wondered if she could cook, then he wondered if she was the virtuous woman the he needed in his life.

"Do you speak Japanese?"

She just looked at him and grinned.

"Is that a wrong question to ask?" he asked looking a

little confused and thought it may have something to do with their destination.

"No not at all," she said as she started standing up gathering her purse. "Let's head on out."

Rebeccah never told him about the languages she could speak, if she had spoken any others at all. When they stepped out of the jet, there was a red carpet on the ground and another limo. The man standing next to the car looked like the same driver that had taken his car to his condo. He thought that could not have happened especially since there would have been no way he could have made it there before them. They had gotten into the limo and a question had crossed Brian's mind. "I know that you do not like people in your business as you mentioned before, but can I know something about you so that I know that you are really real, and that this is not a dream."

Rebeccah pondered a second before she decided to answer, which was when the limo started to move. "You know, in my line of work I come across people that are hard for me to trust. Ever since I was a child, I have had issues with trusting a lot of people. I never stayed with my parents that often. They were busy entertaining and I grew up around my nanny more than them. I felt as though I was not protected by them like most kids my age were by their parents. When I had events at school, I would always look out in the audience to see if they would be there. I would always see other kids with their families, but the only person that I had would be my nanny and sometimes that would only be after and not during a recital. She wouldn't be there through the entire event most times. Then when I grew up and started my very first business, which was a small record label, I had a business partner that took everything I had invested into the company. I lost my money, contacts, everything. You know its funny you are the first person I ever shared that with. I guess I feel comfortable with you."

She looked over at Brian and could see that he felt a little sorry for her. She didn't mind. He had allowed her to just be herself without any major questions. He allowed her to open up when she felt like it, which made her relax even more. "You sure are silent over there."

"No not silent, I am just giving you my full attention. I find it better to listen, than to judge."

"Hhm. You know it's funny."

"What's that?"

"I have always been judged my entire life. If not by others, by myself. I guess you can say that I am very hard on myself."

"To tell you the truth, I am the same way. You know it's hard for someone like me to be in front of so many people and not be judged. I feel the majority of the time though, that I am my worse critic."

"I guess we have a lot in common then," she realized that he seemed like a nice patient man. She could tell by his look that he had gone through a lot in his life. She didn't want to pry into his personal business, she was just supposed to apologize to him and move on. She didn't really think anything else about a future with him. It was better that they kept everything minimal.

"I will say this, Brian. Yes I do know how to speak Japanese, along with three other languages. I guess you can say four additional languages."

"And what are they?"

"Spanish, French, and Greek," she said while looking out of her window. "It looks like we are at our destination."

"Wait. What's the fourth language," he asked reminding her that she had missed one.

"Oh ghetto," she said with a little chuckle. She had to ease up for the moment to prepare him for what was to come. He seemed to have enjoyed it because he laughed uncontrollably.

Rebeccah is really cute, educated and funny Brian surmised. He liked that about her. She really had him going there for a minute, but when he thought about it, ghetto was a form of language. She was funny and so far every quality in her that he had seen, he was pleased with.

"You may have to share your slang with me one day."

"Oh no problem. You may see it when we get out of the limo."

He was a little worried when she made that comment. He thought she had a concert planned with some of her artist. He did not know where she had taken him until he finally noticed what was outside of his window. "Rebeccah, you did not do this," he said in amazement.

"Do what?"

"Bring me to the greatest place on earth."

"Ha-Ha. I knew you would like it."

When they had gotten out of the car, he had seen the big roller coaster that reminded him of his childhood. He loved Disneyland and he didn't know how she was able to pull it off, but she did.

"How did you know this was my favorite spot?"

"I have connections in high places, remember."

"Call me crazy but, Disneyland was a place I always enjoyed being at as a child. I remember coming here once or twice when my parents were together. When they separated I was sixteen and it was real hard on me. The one thing that I remembered that always made me happy was Disneyland. Everything at that time was joyous. Life at home was peaceful, no arguing, hatred, or anything of that nature. I don't want to be forward, but why did you bring me here?"

"Because, I felt that I was way too rude to you before. I figured that you had been going through some hard times lately and that you needed to relax, so what better place to do that then Disneyland. Here you do not have to be a preacher, teacher, or counselor. Here you can be yourself."

Brian was really falling for Rebeccah. He wondered how could she be so caring and go the extreme like she did without wanting anything in return. *God is she the one for me. She has all the qualities, she is even beautiful, and I wonder if she could cook.*

"Girl you can make a man go crazy," he stated. *Why are you single still, Ms. Rebeccah?*

"Yes," she said to him like a little kid wanting to go have fun.

"Can you cook?"

"Can I cook? That's like asking a skinny woman does she not eat. Brian, you do not know the half of it. The evening is still young so we will talk about eating later. Come on, let's go enjoy ourselves."

And that they did.

Thank you God for sending her my way.

Chapter
6

Brian had not had as much fun as he did that evening with Rebeccah in his life. He noticed that she did know how to have a good time. He had almost forgotten how old he was because of the way he would run to each ride as if he were a little child all over again. Everything felt like it was meant to be; perfect. They went from one ride to another not having to wait in lines like the other people did. They ate 'til they had gotten full and even took a few pictures with Mickey and Minnie Mouse. He could see himself spending the rest of his life with her. He even imagined them bringing their children and grandchildren to the place where he fell in love with the woman that he felt should be his wife. He wondered how long it would have to take for a courtship to be okay in God's eyes. He didn't want the evening to end. Especially after the fireworks show, which was an indication that the park was closing. He wanted the rest of his days to be just the same when he was with her, relaxed and okay just being himself without any qualms or heirs.

"Did you have a good time?" she asked while they were walking to the limo.

"Did I have a good time? Girl, you have no idea. I was just thinking about how wonderful this was."

"I can tell by that picture of you on Space Mountain that you were a little scared."

"Sweetie, I wasn't scared I can tell ya that much. I was just worried about you."

"Yeah uhm-hhm sure you were."

"I wasn't."

"If you say so. But that picture said it all. You looked like you were holding on for dear life."

"No, what about you laughing the entire ride?"

"I get that way when I get a little nervous."

"It's cute, but *I* on the other hand wasn't scared."

"Yes you were."

"Okay maybe just a little, but it was still fun."

"Good. I hope you are ready for more."

"More what?"

"You'll see."

"I don't have any other clothes and the ones I have on are drenching wet from the water ride."

"Don't worry. I have everything under control."

"Do you really now?"

"Yes, that I do."

"Are you always in control?"

"Only when I have to be."

"Good." It was good for Brian to see that she was willing to at least give up some control in her life. He never suspected that he would meet his match. Most women he would meet didn't equal up to his standards, but Rebeccah was that and then some, for him. She was on an entirely different level. *Lord thank you again for bringing her into my life. I never thought that I would meet my match.* He thought a little harder and wondered what could be wrong with her. He couldn't put his finger on it, but when he was around her she seemed familiar to him. It didn't bother her when he held her hand when they walked through the shops and around the park. He was truly happy.

"Rebeccah?" he asked while they were in the limo headed to their next destination. He didn't even care anymore where they were headed, just as long as he was in her presence.

"Yes, Brian?"

"How come a woman such as yourself, who seems perfect in every way, is not with someone?"

"I wouldn't go as far as saying that I am perfect, but I chose to be single. I never found someone that understood me. Most men I come across want to control me or are afraid of who I am. They think that since I have so much money, I am hard to handle. In retrospect, I am just like everyone else who wants to be happy."

"I call it as I see it, and in my eyes, you are perfect."

"Well thank you for the complement."

"You're welcome."

"Brian, may I ask you something?"

"Sure, why not."

"How come a man with your accomplishments is still single? You seem like you would be with someone right now."

"I have to be cautious of who I spend my time with. Remember, I am still a preacher and who I bring into my life has to know and love God as much as I do. The woman in my life has to be just as strong in her faith as I am. She also has to be able to handle being with a preacher."

"I guess she will have some big shoes to fill, huh?"

"Not necessarily, but she does have to know that God is always first in my life. Then my family comes second. A woman has to be drama free. It would be nice if she didn't have children, but that is hard to find now of days. So whatever God sends my way, I will know."

"How will you know? Will the angels sing from heaven?"

"Not really like that, but I will know."

"Seriously, how will you know?"

"Love is something that you can not actually define.

The *phileo*, which is shared from one person to another, is very important. Since you know Greek you understand that right?"

"Phileo is love from one person to another who is of the opposite sex, like brotherly love."

"Right! Well, I will say that that kind of love is longsuffering, kind, does not promote itself, is not presented in an unbecoming manner, not easily provoked, is not unrighteous, finds the best in all, and does not seek its own thing."

"Isn't that just like the fruits of the Spirit?"

He had to look at her twice to make sure he was not dreaming. "How do you know about that?"

"Just because I don't always attend a church still doesn't mean I don't know about the Bible."

"You amaze me you know that?"

"And why is that?"

"You just do. Pinch me real quick."

"*What?*"

"Pinch me because this seems like a dream that I do not want to wake up from."

"You're so silly."

They finally made it up to the driveway that Rebeccah was so familiar with. She had just been in Brentwood the previous month. The west coast home of hers excited her every time she would ride up the driveway. It was hard for her to believe that the mansion that stood before her was something that she owned and paid for with cash. The home was her first one that she purchased several years prior. It had seven baths, eight bedrooms, maids' quarters, pool, sauna, and the works. She loved her California home. When they had driven through the gates it made her love it even more. She enjoyed Tennessee but something about California always made her light up. She guessed she had been grinning real hard because Brian noticed.

"Why are you so happy?"

"I was thinking about how thankful I am to have the things that I have obtained."

"What do you mean?"

"Welcome to my home away from home, Mansion Hill," She said as she rolled down her windows to get a full view of her large home.

"Is this you?"

"Yes sir! All 25,000 Square feet."

"This isn't you, girl!"

"But it is."

"I guess you are right. I am amazed every time I learn something new about you."

"My life isn't really exciting as it is to others. I have accumulated so much but yet and still I am missing something. Someone to enjoy and share all of this with," she said realizing no one had time for neither her nor her antics.

The limo pulled up to the front and a tall man opened the limo door.

"Welcome home, Ms. Carpenter."

"Thank you, Daniel. This is our house guest Brian Foster so if he needs anything ,show him around."

"That I will do, ma'am."

"Pleased to meet you brother," Brian said while trying to give the butler a ghetto handshake.

"Do you have any luggage, sir?" Daniel asked feeling a little embarrassed for the houseguest.

"They are all in the car, Daniel. If you can take them to the royal room that will be fine."

"Yes ma'am."

"Royal room?! What kind of set up do you have

here?"

"Oh it's just another home to me."

"How do you have time to stay here and enjoy it?"

"Most of the time I don't. I usually rent it out for studio productions and so forth."

"You can rent a house out like this?"

"But of course, honey. Welcome to L.A. Anything and everything can be rented here."

"This is just so different from the life that I am used to."

"You get used to it after awhile, but it does get lonely every now and again."

"Let me show you to your room real quick and then I will check on you in about thirty minutes."

"But I didn't bring anything except for what I have on now and my suit, remember?"

"I remember. But you know what, Brian, sometimes you should relax a little and have faith that everything will work out just fine."

"Ok you got me there."

"You aren't tired are you?"

"No not at all, even though it is about 1am back home. How do you do it?"

"Do what?"

"Come from a meeting in Japan, fly to LA to Disneyland, and still not be tired?"

"I don't know. I run on some kind of fuel. It's hard for me to sleep anyway. I have so many things on my mind that I can not keep track of the time. When I am tired I fall out for hours. I really don't think about it much."

"You are something else."

"If you say so. I am just an average woman who works hard."

"Not really average by any account, Rebeccah."

"I guess I have forgotten what average was, but in my

mind I felt like I was a go getter who could achieve anything that I wanted in life. Here's your room, the royal suite. The bathroom is over there to your right and the walk in closet is next to it."

As she walked towards the closet, she noticed that her staff had taken care of everything that she asked them to do. She noticed the few things from the list that Candice faxed over and was pleased. She turned to Brian.

"You have a few clothes in here they should fit you just right; I sent one of my assistants out to buy them for you. Let me know if the clothes will do. The towels and everything are in the restroom. Of course here is your bed. And if you need anything you can pick up the phone here and it will go directly to one of the butlers or maids."

"Man, you have to pinch me again because this is really just far beyond reality for me right now."

"Reality, honey? This is still just the half of it," she said as she began walking away to go to her room.

"Rebeccah," Brian said to her before she could leave out.

"Yes?"

"Thank you again for such a wonderful time. No one has ever done anything like this for me at all in my life."

"Not a problem, Brian. I guess I can consider you a friend now and friends take care of one another."

"So true."

"I'll be back in thirty minutes to give you a mini tour."

The next morning, Brian had awakened thinking about the mini tour Rebeccah had given him of her mansion. He noticed how immaculate it was. She didn't show him every room nor did he see hers. which was good. He didn't want to be falsely accused of anything later. The mansion was completely laid out; she even had her own studio, which was near the pool area. The night before, they stayed up and watched movies in her home theatre.

While he sat there in bed, he started feeling a little guilty for not being at home and at the church. He thought about what everyone would think if they knew that he had slept in the same house as a single woman. It wasn't like they were in the same room, but people still assumed the worse. *"Why am I tripping? She and I were not in the same bed together at all. She is still a single woman and I am a single man and that wouldn't look right."* After battling with himself, he felt he should call the church to see how everything was going. His bed in the royal suite was plush. He had never slept so well before in his life. Everything had down feathers in it from the pillows to the comforter. Nothing was out of place nor was it out of order. He said his morning prayers and thought about how her assistant had picked out some fine clothes for him to wear. Everything was name brand and was the right size, which meant they fit just right. Before watching movies, they ended up going to some small restaurant to eat. She finally fell asleep on the large theatre chair around four in the morning.

He reached to grab his cell phone on top of the nightstand. It was now one in the afternoon in Tennessee. *Lord this life is lovely, well not the lifestyle but the things you have allowed her to be a steward over while she is working. She doesn't talk about you much, Father. I wonder if she will eventually think of you as being head of her life.*

"The Holy Tabernacle of God, praise God and Good afternoon this is Sister Jenkins speaking. How may I help you?"

"Good morning, Sister…"

"And how are you this fine afternoon, Pastor

Foster?"

"Just fine and you, Sister Jenkins?"

"I am just blessed."

"You know you and I need to talk when I get back don't you?"

"I am not sure what you are talking about. Is your phone losing its signal?"

"No, Sister Jenkins. It isn't losing signal. I am sure you know why I called this morning?"

"Yes sir actually I do. I hope you are enjoying your trip. When my niece Candice called me and said that Ms. Rebeccah wanted to apologize, I thought that that was the best thing for you to do."

"But Sister Jenkins you know I have Bible study tonight."

"Sometimes, brother, the Lord understands. Besides, I saw how you looked at her the first time you saw her practicing with the choir. Your eyes lit up like a little child who had seen his mother for the first time."

He knew he didn't act that way when he had first seen Rebeccah. At least he didn't think he did. Sister Jenkins did put him in a predicament where he would have to do a lot of explaining if anyone found out about why he left. He guessed she had his best interest at heart because she did treat him as if he was her own, and he loved her for that.

"Who is going to teach the…"

"Now don't you worry your head about that? You are out there on a vacation and if anyone asks why you are away, I will tell them that you are out there in California on business for the church."

"But that isn't going to work…"

"You are out there on business trying to bring more people closer to the Lord."

"But Sister…"

"There will be no more buts young man. Take it from

me, I know love when I see it so let God do the rest and everything else will work out just fine. I have to go someone is here to fix the hot water heater. You enjoy yourself now."

"Yes ma'am," was all he could say. Maybe she was right that he needed to move out of the way, stop worrying, and let the Lord take control. Brian felt that if Rebeccah and he were meant to be, it would all work out on its own. He heard a knock at the door.

"Come in."

"Good morning, sir. I hope I didn't wake you."

"Nah, Daniel. Not at all, man."

"Good sir. You are requested by Ms Rebeccah to have brunch in twenty minutes by the pool."

"Say man, let me ask you something from one brother to another."

"Yes sir, what is that?"

"You can just call me Brian, man."

"Ok Brian, sir."

"How often does Rebeccah do this for her friends?"

"Hardly ever sir... I mean Brian, sir."

"Did she say why she invited me here?"

"Whatever Ms. Rebeccah does is her own business. I work for her and rarely do I ask questions."

"Ok, man. I guess you helped me out a little."

"Will there be anything else that you need, sir."

"Nah man, that's it for now. Thanks."

"No problem, sir. Your robe and house slippers are next to the bed when you are ready to go downstairs."

"Thanks, man." Brian knew at one point in time Daniel struggled on the streets just like he did. Brian allowed the streets to raise him. He hustled just like everyone else. He had to survive and his mother and younger sister had to eat. Things weren't so easy for him after his parents separated. He knew he wanted to be more than what he was growing up to become. He always strived to live like Rebeccah back in

Tennessee. To see her kind of lifestyle in action was amazing but sad. With all of the things she had around her, she was still lonely. She seemed like she really didn't have anyone around to trust or talk to. Everyone was a 'yes man.' He didn't get that on the streets. Every man had to gain respect, earn it, and they all knew who to cross and not to. With her, everyone seemed to treat her as if she was just a boss and not a friend. He felt he knew her a little more and his heart went out to her. She hustled just like he did as a teenager in order to survive.

The only difference was, he slanged rocks and she slanged music and ideas.

As he walked down the granite staircase, he couldn't help but think about how hard it was for a woman to feel secure in a life as hers. How could she be happy?

She was a lot like him even though they were in different places in their lives. As he walked near the pool, which he could see through the double pain doors, he could hear someone in the kitchen. The food smelled just like that good old-fashioned home cooking down south. He peeped around the corner to find Rebeccah working over the hot stove. She didn't look like she was lost in her own kitchen. She seemed comfortable working as if she had been cooking for years. She was squeezing fresh orange juice, frying some bacon and sausage, making pancakes, and omelets that she was about to get started on. She noticed him standing in the kitchen doorway

"Good morning, Brian. I hope you slept well," she said while smiling and looking even more amazing to him.

God this is so difficult for me. Maybe Sister Jenkins was right. I need to just go with the flow and let You do all the work and enjoy what You have provided for me. "Yes I slept well thank you."

"I'm glad. I was hoping that bed would be fitting enough for you."

"Everything was nice. Just perfect," he said as he

started walking towards the counter. "Do you need help with anything?"

"Oh no. I have it. Just make yourself at home by the pool and I will be out there shortly."

"Ok," he said while admiring her. He wanted to tell her right then and there that he loved her, but he knew that it was not the right time, nor place, for it. He knew that he needed to take his time, wait, and work on being patient. *Father, guide me to be patient and do the things that is best fitting and acceptable in Your site.*

He walked out the sliding doors toward the table by the pool. He noticed the view from her home on top of the hill was breath taking. He never really noticed how big and wonderful God was until he was right in His presence. The Lord was around when he least expected it. The ocean on one side and the mountains behind him. He thought that only one Lord could create something that was so beautiful.

"I hope you have an appetite, Brian."

"It sure smells good and looks fantastic."

"Why thank you, sir. I can burn a little."

She sat down across from him while one of the maids served them. Brain enjoyed the delicious food but more importantly for the first time in his life, he really felt what he had preached about for several years. He felt true unconditional love.

―――――――

"I can't ride back with you, Brian. I have a bit of business that I need to take care of out here. But I will be back home in a few days," Rebeccah said while walking Brian out to the limo. She didn't notice that they had been holding hands again, but she felt so safe with him.

"It has really been a pleasure and I am thankful for

you opening up your home and spending time with me. Your apology is greatly accepted."

"I'm glad you enjoyed it and next time you owe me one."

"I don't know if I could live up to this, but I would be honored if we could do something like this again. I may not have the long money that you have, but it's the thought that counts, right?"

"But of course it is."

He reached over and gave her a hug to say thank you. For a minute there, she had begun to think the wrong thing and pulled herself away from him quickly. "You enjoy your trip home."

"I will. I hate that you can't join me on the way back."

"There will be other times I am sure."

"Bye, Reebie" he said as he gave her a soft kiss on her cheek. She could see herself with someone like him. She knew she would have to change her lifestyle but didn't want do that right away. There was still money for her to make and things for her to do. She needed to call Terry and Kathy and tell them about her day out with the preacher man. As she walked in the door of the mansion she realized that for once, it was good having someone other than her staff at her home. The parties were okay, but everyone was on another level; one where it was about using her for something. With Brian, he was nice company to have around. He brought back life into her home and she guessed a little bit into her heart as well.

This was the most she had ever done for a male. Normally they wined and dined her; all for the wrong reasons. She had to apologize to Brian, however, for how wrong she treated him and she hoped it was a lasting impression with him. When she approached her kitchen she noticed that she was standing in the same spot where Brian was watching her from a few hours earlier. It surprised her for a minute when she looked up and noticed him watching her make breakfast. She then realized that he enjoyed watching her. She wasn't sure how long he had been standing there, but she did know that he enjoyed watching her cook. While they were having breakfast poolside, he explained to her that most women the he knew would go out to eat all the time. They didn't know their way around a kitchen at all.

They didn't know that cooking was one of the criteria for being a woman. He also explained to her that females who did cook meals for him at the church to get on his good side would bring him plates and bowls of food that wasn't really good enough for anyone to eat. He even told her that one lady went as far as buying something from a restaurant and put it in a casserole dish like she cooked it herself. She put it in the bag that she purchased the meal from and left the receipt at the bottom. She claimed she cooked it for him but after he read the items on the receipt that were on his plate, he knew better than to believe her again.

Brian was a very humble guy who had a sense of humor. She learned a lot about him. She found out that he was the oldest child, which he had told her the night before over dinner. He also told her that when he went to seminary school, he had gotten into a little bit of trouble. He never would tell her exactly what had happened, but after he had gotten into trouble, he knew not to make the same mistake anymore and that he shouldn't play with God. Brian said that every now and again he would go to a jazz club or if he had the opportunity, he would go dancing. She found it odd that a preacher would do all of that. She surmised they were just like everyone else after she and he finished talking. Her idea was totally misguided, but Brian had shed a new light on the topic of being a preacher.

She stood by her barstool and all she could think about was how he made her feel at ease. She didn't fall for men like him before so quickly. "I can't fall for a man like this," she said out loud. Something about him soothed her spirit, even thinking about him made her feel at ease. The phone rang and brought her back from her idea of being in love.

"Hello?"

"Hello again, Ms. Lady."

"Say, is everything okay, Brian?"

"Everything is just wonderful. I just wanted to call you back again and tell you thank you and that I am keeping you in my prayers."

"You're welcome and I am going to do the same."

"Thank you and I'll hold you to your promise that you will allow me to do the same for you when you come home."

"Of course I will," she said smiling like a teenager who first felt the joy in having a guy call her.

"Well, I am going to let you go 'cause I know how busy you are. But I will definitely see you on Saturday right?"

"That you will," she said not wanting to let him hang up the phone and realized that she was being childish. "I'll talk to you later."

"Okay. Bye."

"Bye," she said knowing that Brian had her real quick. She didn't know why she was feeling the way she was. "Whatever you have me going through please don't hurt me later." *Please God let this man be the one.*

She sat down on the stool and watched one of her maids, Maria, clean the stove. She looked at the phone and thought about calling Terry to let him in on all the details.

"Maria, that will be all for now."

"Are you sure Ms.?"

"Yes I am sure. I will finish up in here."

"Okay if you say so. You have gone a little crazy since that man was here. Making breakfast, inviting him over. I would say you are in love with him."

"Maria."

"I am just saying. He seemed to me like a nice man. He made you happy."

"How do you know?"

"Because you are still smiling."

"No I am not," she said and then caught herself. She and Maria went way back. She was the first person that Rebeccah hired when she purchased her mansion. Rebeccah use to hang out with her daughter Leticia on a couple of occasions. Leticia had even worked for her at the label until she had gotten married.

"How is Leti?"

"Big like a balloon."

"She's pregnant, again?"

"Yeah and I can't wait to see you walking around with a little mejito."

"Give it time. I just met the guy, tia," she called her that on occasion. Maria was like an auntie to Rebeccah. She was a very sweet older lady that knew how to have a good time on or off the clock. She was there when Rebeccah went through all the bad publicity, men, and drama in her life. She would just hold her in her arms and rock her back and forth like a little child and would hum an old Spanish tune to make Rebeccah relax after doing so much crying.

"I'll clean up. Just relax yourself for awhile."

"Odios Mios! You have lost your mind for sure. Do you have a fever or something," she said while feeling Rebeccah's forehead. "He has really brightened up your day. What is the world coming to? He's a keeper mija."

"Thank you for your approval," she said as Maria walked out of the kitchen. She was a funny lady Rebeccah thought. Very honest and didn't hold back a thing. Rebeccah picked up the phone and dialed Terry's number.

"All praises to God this is, Terry. How may I help you?"

"Terry, are you okay?"

"But of course, child. I am much better than ok."

"You could have fooled me by the way you answered the phone."

"The way I answered? I always answer this way. You just never pay attention."

"You do? I never knew that. Hhm. But anyway, check this out. I have something to share with you and I don't want you to get overly excited."

"What did you do now?"

"I didn't do anything!"

"Are you sure?"

"Yes I am sure, Terry. Will you just listen?"

"Okay, okay, but how did your meeting go in Japan?"

"That was fine, but that isn't what I called you about."

"Okay child, I'm listening. Shoot."

"Well, remember when I told you that I was a bit rude to Brian. I mean the preacher?"

"What are you on first name basis with him now?"

"Be quite. Do you remember?"

"Yes I remember."

"Well, I wanted to apologize to him for being so harsh because you know how I can get?"

"Boy do I!"

"Do you want to hear this or what?"

"Yes I do. Will you go on, girl."

"Well, I flew him out here to LA and we had the time of our lives."

"You did what?!" he said a little shocked.

"Calm down, just calm down. I didn't hurt the poor man. We didn't go out to a club or anything like that."

"That's good, praise Jesus. But how did all of this happen?"

As she began telling Terry the story, she started

feeling lonely that Brian wasn't there with her. She was also excited because it had been a long time since she had ever felt the way she did about anyone. Terry had been at complete attention when she told him about the visit to Disneyland and the late dinner. He was even shocked that Candice and her aunt had hooked Rebeccah up with the information she needed to know about Brian.

"I knew it! I knew it!"

"You knew what?"

"I knew that he was the one for you."

"But I do not see myself being with a preacher."

"This is the time for courtship honey, not something you can rush and let happen over night. This is much different than being with a pro ball player, rapper, or actor."

"I know that. What, you think I can't handle this?"

"Of course you can handle it, honey. But now you have to be even more prepared. When you get home we are going to have to do some work honey, to make you look fierce for your husband to be."

"My what!? See you have gone way too far?"

"Don't sit there and act like you haven't thought of that already."

"It was just an apology *thank you* kind of meeting."

"Honey, that was not a meeting. *That* is the Lord working."

"Look! Why do you…"

"See, we have to work on you and your acceptance to God for now. Honey, I have a meeting I have to go to but when you get back home baby, we are going to do some things."

"Terry, don't share this with everyone from the church. I want to take my time with it."

"Girl, you don't have to worry about that. Terry has your back. Just hurry up and get home so Kathy and I can walk you through some things. I gotta go sweetie, okay?"

"Okay."

"Bye girl. Hallelujah and praise Jesus."

"Uhm, ok, bye," Rebeccah didn't know how obnoxious Terry could be at times. She wondered what he had planned up his sleeves. She also wondered how he knew that she and Brian would make a good couple.

"Here I go again talking like he and I are dating. Whatever it is, I am feeling a bit happy about it," she said out loud.

"Rebeccah," her assistant called.

"Yes, Quinn?"

"You have to start getting ready for the release party."

"Ok, honey. I'm moving." She had finished cleaning the stove while she was on the phone with Terry. She even did the last of the dishes that could not fit in the dishwasher. She couldn't believe how she was handling herself, as if she was already in wife mode. If she were to court Brian, she was not going to be able to go to release parties.

"Time to get all dolled up and be an LA beauty. Let's see, Mrs. Rebeccah Elise Foster. Kind of has a nice ring to it," she said while walking up the stairs. "What am I doing? I need to keep my mind on my music business and not on Brian."

She thought it did have a nice ring to it and grinned before entering into her room.

Chapter
7

Brian finally made it home and his car keys were in his condo. He didn't know how they had gotten there, but it brought his mind back to Rebeccah and how much planning she had done to make everything eventful. He then remembered that Sister Jenkins had a spare key to his condo. "That is a sneaky sister" he said while walking to his room. He loved Mama Jenkins though.

On the flight back home, Brian couldn't help but think of being with Rebeccah and living in the lifestyle that she was accustomed to. Everything in his eyes was perfect. She even had good taste in picking out clothes for him. Then he thought at least her assistant went out and purchased them for her, but he was sure that Rebeccah picked out the items on her own. He smiled because Rebeccah was a *tough* woman. She spoke five different languages, had her own jet, traveled across the globe, she was the total package. He was a little upset that he didn't get to hear her speak her fourth language. He loved walking alongside her and being with her at the theme park. He couldn't wait to see her again on Saturday.

He was at peace and could tell she was relaxed around him as well. She was everything he had asked the Lord for and then some. He thought it would be a problem with the differences in professions. He was familiar with the music that her label had put out. None of it was acceptable for the life of a preacher. "Who am I fooling? It would be hard for a woman like that to leave that kind of life that she is comfortable with. I wouldn't be able to provide for her the things that she likes or needs. I only have one thing to offer and that would be my love. Maybe that is all she really needs. I can still see how someone of her status could be very lonely," he said while looking around his condo.

He thought about the limo ride and the conversation that they had about her childhood. He could tell that she grew up pretty lonely. Not having one parent around for him was hard, but for her not seeing either one had to have been even tougher.

As he reminisced in his sofa he glanced at the clock. Brian still had enough time to make it to church for Wednesday night Bible study. He was going to sit in the back and observe since there would be someone else running the program. Sometimes he felt that he was better at watching and listening than standing in front of everyone and doing what he did best, preaching. He thought that it would be better that he sat and learned because Rebeccah and the night before was still on his mind and it would have been hard for him to concentrate on trying to teach someone something. From the breakfast, Disneyland to her entire demeanor, Brian was pleased. He could tell what Sister Jenkins had said was true. If he let go and let God take care of the rest, everything would fall into place. It seemed to him like both he and Rebeccah were one and everything that he had felt was perfect in every way.

As Brian had gotten into his Range Rover, he couldn't help but think about how it would be nice to have a driver every now and again like Rebeccah had instead of driving around all the time. He already had it planned out in his mind about courting her, which he knew would take some time before he would initiate the idea with her. Her lifestyle would have to be different in order for her to be by his side. He was a firm believer in putting the Lord first in everything that he did. A life of hip-hop music and music videos would not suffice and he would have to ease Rebeccah into the right way of living.

When he pulled into the parking lot, low and behold, Lesha was standing outside the church in his parking spot acting as if she was looking for someone. Brian figured that she made it back from her trip, but wasn't really concerned about her one bit. Lesha was the total opposite of what a virtuous woman should be. She did not even *touch* the qualities of what Rebeccah had. Lesha had no class, was very flamboyant, loud, and ghetto. And the way she dressed was completely wrong. She could take a few tips from Rebeccah. The first thing that she would need to learn is being classy, but the idea of Lesha having class was a stretch.

"Hello, Brian," she said while walking up to his door and opening it before he could even get out.

"Hello, Sister."

"Well you certainly look nice this evening. You bought a new outfit I see."

"This is just a little something that I had," he wanted to know why he was even explaining any of it to her.

"I didn't think you were going to make it. When Sister Jenkins said that you were out of town on business, I thought I wouldn't be able to see you and it kind of broke my heart. But now that you are here, everything is fine and I am much better."

"As you can see I am here now," he said a little upset with her while she was trying to gather his things out of his car for him. "How may I help you this evening?"

"You have a short attitude today. What has gotten you all bothered?"

He wanted to tell her that she had him bothered, but he didn't. He didn't want to ruin his thoughts from the previous day and instead changed his attitude even though she *was* bothering him. "I apologize for the attitude I just have a lot on my mind, Sister," he explained thinking to himself that once again she was nowhere near his thoughts.

"Oh well, if you need me for *anything* you know I am here for you, Brian," she said while brushing up against him and putting something in his pants pocket.

"Whoa, whoa Sister," he said trying to dodge away but he couldn't go too far because she had him pinned against his truck. "That's a little too close for comfort."

"Hhm if you say so, Brian. Call me if you need anything," she said with an evil grin as she started to walk into the church.

God please bless this woman with a man so that she will not bother me anymore. As he made it into his office, he noticed a package on his desk with a card attached to it.

> *Brian,*
>   *Thank you again for such a wonderful evening. I really enjoyed myself. I hope you did as well.*
>   *Reebie…*

To his surprise, it was a box of his favorite chocolates from a chocolate candy chain in California.

"How did this make it here before I did? This is one tough woman," he said out loud.

A knock at the door brought him back from his mini vacation.

"Pastor, May I come in?"

"Sure Sister Jenkins, sure," he said with a slight grin.

"You seem very relaxed."

"I had the best time ever, momma. It was something that I really needed."

"I hope you didn't mind my interfering, but like I told you on the phone my niece was very persistent and I could tell you wanted, or shall I say needed, some time to spend with her to get to know her a little better."

"Thank you Sister," he said opening the box of chocolates. "Would you like some chocolates?"

"Oh why sure. Thank you, brother. Was everything fine?"

"Everything was fine, Mama Jenkins, and then some. I never knew that I can still enjoy myself and not have to worry about anything else but the moment. She has really captivated me."

"Uh-oh! Do I hear love in the air?"

"I wouldn't go that far, but I will say that I have met my match."

She looked at him while taking a bite of chocolate not believing that he could not be in love. She read him like a book, but decided to let it rest.

"Love does not happen that fast does it?"

"Well you have a little twinkle in your eye and you're smiling like a little child who's found his favorite toy. You never know what God has in store for you."

"Excuse me again, Brain," Lesha said barging into his office, "but did you get the note I left in your pocket?"

Brian assumed that she had been standing outside of the door getting her ear hustle on. It wasn't a coincidence that she would show up right when she did; which again was the wrong time. He could see that Sister Jenkins was a little upset with her, too. Lesha had a look of want in her eyes for Brian and she wouldn't stop at anything to satisfy her need. Regardless of how bad she looked in the process.

"Oh some chocolates for me? Don't mind if I do," she said reaching for the box that was sitting on the edge of Brian's desk. Luckily Sister Jenkins grabbed the card that Lesha was about to pick up and dared her to even think about taking it out of her hand.

"Now you know if he didn't offer those to you, you should at least ask, silly girl."

"Brian knows me. He knows I don't have to ask him for anything, right Brian?"

Brian didn't understand her angle at all. At the rate she was working, she would not be able to keep any man because she would possibly smother him to death. Again he thought of Rebeccah and began to smile again because she was the definition of a perfect woman for him.

"Why you smiling so hard? Are you thinking about you and I together finally?"

"Sister Walker! I think we need to leave now so that the Pastor can take care of some things. He's been busy taking care of business, so we have to give him his privacy."

"That better be all he was doing was taking care of church business."

"Girl, if your father knew how you could be sometimes."

"Whatever mean woman! Brian, read the letter when you get a chance."

He waved her off as if to say yes okay but what he was really thinking was that letter she gave him would never be read. *Lord, forgive me but she is not right at all in the brain.*

Brian had gotten a lot out of Bible study. For some odd reason, Deacon Hawkins was speaking on relationships within the church. Brian wondered if he knew about his trip to California. When he started teaching, Sister Jenkins looked at Brian as if to say don't worry no one knew their little secret. The conclusion Brian had gathered from the lesson though was that the Lord was working both on he and Rebeccah. He was giving them a chance to work on something major. As long as they let Him take control of the entire relationship, everything would be fine.

When Brian made it home, he changed into his usual home attire, which was his shorts, jersey and house slippers. The note that Lesha had given to him earlier had fallen out of his pocket onto the floor. He opened it up and had noticed for one, that the girl could not spell at all. And for two, he couldn't imagine how anyone like herself could be so obvious and ignorant at the same time.

> *Dear Brian,*
>
> *It seems to me that you are not sure of what you want and need in your life. I am the girl that can give you every thang you have evah desired and more. I have loved you from tha first time I saw you and I new that you would be tha man for me. stop playin' around and gave me a call cause this gril is ready, willing, and able to make this worth your wile.*
>
> *Signed your gril and potential wife,*
> *Lesha Walker-Foster*

"Oh my God how could she be so crazy? Lord please guide this woman away from me 'cause I am not wanting her in my life at all." He threw away the letter and went to the living room a little disgusted by what he had just read. He wondered what made her think that he wanted her or even needed her in his life. As he looked down at his coffee table, he noticed the copy of SouthSyde Magazine with Rebeccah on the cover.

"This, Dear Lord, is my type. I wonder if I should call her. Nah. I shouldn't do that," he said remembering that Rebeccah had told him she had a release party to go to. Then he thought he should text her to let her know the he had made it home safely.

Chapter
8

Reebie,

Thank you for the chocolates again you amaze me. I made it home safely thanks again.

Brian F.

Rebeccah was not expecting a message from Brian that evening. She had gotten home twenty minutes after making an appearance at the release party. She didn't feel right being in the LA crowd, which was unusual for her. She contemplated that she could have been sick, but then rethought the idea. That night she didn't even do any drinking. Everyone at the party didn't make her feel at peace like she did when she was with Brian. She wondered if he was still awake.

"Imma call him," she said while sitting on her sofa. She picked up her two-way sidekick and dialed his number.

"Hello?"

"Hello, Miss Lady," Brian said in his mellow voice. "I was just thinking about you."

"You were now, were you?"

"Yes, that I was."

"Quite as it's kept, I was doing the same."

"What's that? Thinking about you, too?"

"No silly, about you."

"That's odd, shouldn't you be thinking about that big release party?"

"I didn't stay there long at all. Matter of fact, I have been home now for a good hour. It's weird because I got all dolled up for nothing."

"Did something happen? Is everything okay?" he asked a little worried

"No, nothing happened. Everything was fine. I just didn't feel right being there and I wanted to leave."

"Really now?"

"Yes, really."

That evening Brian and Rebeccah talked for hours upon hours on the phone as if they were sitting right next to one another sharing life stories. Rebeccah noticed how passionate Brian was about Christ. They went over a few things in the Bible and he would ask her questions about what she felt about life, love, and teaching others. He would read different verses and she would listen to hear how he would break it down for her. She would even ask questions about things that she didn't quite understand. He seemed to enjoy sharing his ideology and didn't mind listening to hers. She learned a lot that evening, not just about Brian but also about herself and how happy she would be being with a man who was a Preacher.

It had been over a week and Rebeccah and Brian had been seeing each other as often as their time permitted. They would meet at different restaurants, coffee houses, even to the movies just to spend more time learning about one

another. They would even talk on the phone endlessly about nothing and everything. She'd ask him certain questions from the Bible, a mini Bible study actually, that he enjoyed sharing what he could with her. He also learned from her. He learned the dynamics of operating a business and how caring a woman Rebeccah truly was.

Each day that they would meet and talk, he was thankful to God for all that He had allowed them to go through together. Brian found himself sending her e-grams or a bouquet of flowers just to show her that she was on his mind. He had not taken the Lord out of his life either and was sharing his love for his Father with her. She seemed to be okay with it. So much so that she began spending more time at the church throughout the week. Nonetheless, their time together had still been kept a secret from those who were at the church. Brian didn't want to make anything public until it was the right time.

He didn't know how to get to the point of officially asking her to date him. He wanted to ask Rebeccah if she would not mind being in a courtship with him, but he was a little afraid of what her reaction would be. For the time being, he liked it the way it was; getting to know one another as friends. He'd love to be with her permanently when, and if, it would get to that point. Brian contemplated on what he would lose if he told her exactly how he felt and if she felt the same way about him. He was never afraid approaching woman when he was younger and running the streets however, during those times he was just living life and not a life for the Lord. He didn't care back then about woman at all; he just used them up. That was until he learned that a woman was an important part to life and creation, a blessing and gift from God. They were not to be controlled or manipulated, but kept, protected, and loved as loving the Lord.

Rebeccah knew that Brian was a busy man and that

the revival was quickly approaching. He could not wait to hear her sing again. Whenever he was in his office during choir rehearsal, he would turn the speakers on when they would practice on her song. After rehearsal, he would find time later in the evening to spend with her or talk with her over the phone.

Brian wanted to surprise Rebeccah with a lunch in the park just because. He wanted to thank her for being such a good inspiration when he doubted himself. She always gave him words of encouragement and would use some of his own words on him, which showed how intently she'd been listening. He knew that there weren't that many women who would actually listen to everything that he would say. Rebeccah would be able to repeat things at different times that he thought in his mind to be insignificant, but to her it was more. Women only listened to Brian only if they wanted something from him. Rebeccah would listen as if he was the only person in the world that was speaking. In return he would do the same.

I am so thankful Lord for you bringing her into my life they way that you have.

Chapter
9

The Courtship Promise Picnic

Now that Brian had been the head pastor at the church for more than two years, knowing that at some point he needed to be married, Rebeccah was the closest thing to being the woman that he felt the Lord wanted him to be with. He battled with the thought quite often about leading the congregation and not being a leader over his own home. Brian knew that in God's time, everything would work out just fine. Women would approach him, but he knew deep in his heart that they were not the one for him. He would talk to a few sisters from the church, even go out to eat or a movie. Other than that, he didn't think much of a companionship with them. He'd pace himself by being patient and knew that all things would work out for the best. He felt his match had finally come into his life. Rebeccah, in his heart, was best for him. He knew deep down that she was his rib and that she completed him.

She was able to complete his thoughts and sentences. Sometimes it would make him chuckle because it scared him a little to see how fast the Lord worked when a void that needed to be filled would appear. Not that he was afraid of God's work one bit, but to see His work in action and the way His blessings appeared made Brian realize how awesome the Lord was. For that very reason, Brian would explain to many of the members that he counseled, that they needed to be careful of what they asked for because anything was possible in the eyes of the Lord. Brian had received exactly what he asked and prayed for, a soul mate.

In order to make the picnic right, he had to ask Sister Jenkins what to take. She was happy for him and wanted the best for him, just like any woman would want for someone close to them. She offered to put together the basket, but Brian insisted that he did it on his own. Rebeccah was someone he had to impress on his own without anyone's help. Mama Jenkins did help Brian with the details, which he didn't mind as much. She brought in a basket that had matching plates, silverware, napkins and glasses. She even thought of the matching blanket and umbrella that they would need.

Mama Jenkins found out from her niece what Rebeccah's favorite colors were, turquoise and brown. Everything that was chosen matched the color palette. What she was also able to obtain from her niece was what food Rebeccah's enjoyed eating for a main course and dessert. Brian was so thankful for having Sister Jenkins and her niece.

The menu consisted of Chicken parmesan, tomato and olive salad with a light vinaigrette, a chocolate mousse topped with raspberries drizzled with chocolate sauce and shaved chocolate, and sparkling cider to drink. He opted for Champaign but didn't want to give her the wrong impression. He wanted to surprise her like she did him.

Candice had everything set up for them as far as her blocking out the schedule for the rest of the day. Brian wanted to make sure that Rebeccah did not have any other meetings or engagements the day of the surprise.

Brian could not wait. He was content with putting together a menu that was pleasing to her, especially since he knew how to burn in the kitchen. He had already gone shopping and everything prepped. He started with the first item on the menu. While utilizing the churches kitchen with

Mama Jenkins available for taste testing, he began with the salad.

Tomato and Olive Salad with a light vinaigrette
3 oz crumbled Feta Cheese
Package of Cherry Tomatoes
Green olives marinated in garlic
Chives
Fresh basil
2tsp olive oil
Salt and pepper to taste

In a bowl he mixed together all of the ingredients and added the salt and pepper to taste. Next, he drizzled the olive oil on top. Finally, he placed them in two fancy bowls that Mama Jenkins purchased for him, and set them in the refrigerator to chill.

The next item on the menu was the Chicken Parmesan. He knew that Rebeccah *loved* Chicken Parmesan with fresh sauce, but he decided to take the easy route in putting it together.

Chicken Parmesan
2 Boneless chicken breast
2 cups bread crumbs seasoned with parmesan cheese
2 tblsp cooking oil
2 tblsp unsalted butter
1 tsp oregano
2 cups spaghetti sauce
Grated mozzarella cheese
Salt and pepper to taste

First, Brian coated the chicken breast with bread crumbs. He had read a recipe that called for dredging the meat but he decided not to. He wanted to make sure the fewer steps he took the better without ruining the taste. In a skillet with both the butter and olive oil, he browned both sides of the chicken breast and then set them on a paper towel to drain off the excess oil. Then Brian put the browned meat in a baking skillet with spaghetti sauce on the bottom, topped the meat with the cheese, moved it to the oven at 400 degrees, and baked it for ten minutes until the mozzarella browned. He finally garnished it with oregano and parmesan cheese. Brian made sure that he kept the meat on warm in the oven and checked every so often so that it would not dry out.

The final item Brian put together was the dessert. He was thankful that she loved chocolate and had an easy desert that he could put together. Mama Jenkins would check in on him every now and again to taste and also to make sure he knew what he was doing. She was pleased to see that he was working so hard in making the picnic extra special for Rebeccah. Without any words, he could tell that she was proud of him. He then started on the chocolate sauce first.

Chocolate sauce
1 cup semisweet chocolate chips
¾ cup whipping cream
1 teaspoon vanilla
¾ teaspoon espresso

He had a small saucepan on the stove with the whipping cream on low heat to melt the chocolate chips. He stirred the mixture constantly until the two melted together. Next, he took it off of the heat and stirred in the vanilla and espresso. When it cooled a little, he poured it into a small container and set it on his prep area until he was ready to drizzle it over the dessert. Next he worked on the grand finale, the mousse.

Chocolate mousse

½ cups sugar
2 tablespoons sugar
¼ cup unsweetened cocoa powder
1 package gelatin (unflavored)
2 cups whipping cream
2 tablespoons espresso
2 egg whites
¼ cup egg substitute
1/8 teaspoon cream of tartar
½ cup whipped topping

Garnish
Shaved chocolate
Raspberries

He combined ½ cup sugar, cocoa powder, and gelatin in a medium saucepan, added the espresso and set it aside for two minutes. He was very meticulous with following the recipe. He cleaned the area until his two minutes was up then turned the burner back on medium heat and stirred it until the sugar and gelatin had dissolved. Brian added the espresso and then stirred in the egg substitute. Next, he took the saucepan off of the burner and set it aside. With each step, all Brian could think about was how happy Rebeccah would be once she tasted his dessert. His heart was warm just thinking of her smile.

In another bowl, he beat the egg whites with the mixture until it was foamy and then added the cream of tartar. Brian started the mixer again until the eggs formed a soft peak. Once the peaks formed, he added the 3 tablespoons of sugar, turned the mixer back on, and waited until he noticed stiff peaks. Brian added the egg white mixture into the cocoa, folded in the whipped topping, and divided the dessert into two wine glasses to refrigerate.

"Mama Jenkins, can you come here for a second

please ma'am?" he asked looking a little puzzled.

"Yes, child. What's wrong? You look bewildered."

"I think I forgot something."

"You didn't forget anything we have it all here."

"Do I look okay?"

"You look fine. Now stop fidgeting and know that everything is going to be okay."

"What about my haircut is it alright?"

"*Yes*, child. Yes."

"I think I might need to change," he said looking at his attire.

"You are fine, son. Just relax and be you. If you can speak in front of hundreds every week, than you can talk to her. It's not like she is a stranger or anything."

"I know, Sister, but I want to make sure everything is perfect."

"The Lords' work is always perfect. Just step out of His way and let Him guide you."

"I guess you are right. But what if she doesn't stay at the office long enough or goes out of town?"

"Hursh chile, hursh. Everything is taken care of. You just mosey on to her office and the Deacons and I will close up the church."

"Yes ma'am," he answered while looking at her to ask one more question.

"Just go, boy. Everything is fine."

He had gotten into the car and noticed that he was shaking a little. He put the basket, blanket, and umbrella in the backseat on the floor. He made sure everything fit tight because he didn't want anything to tip over.

"Calm down, Brian. You can do this man," he told himself while walking around his car.

He then thought about his friend Mike and what he would say if he had seen Brian acting the way he did. Mike would have told him that he was soft or a wimp. Brian hadn't spoken to Mike in a week and a half. He knew that people grew apart form one another and that it was probably time for their friendship to end. Mike was a grown man and didn't need Brain to define his life for him. That life which Mike was accustomed to was the old life for Brian. He had changed and was on his way to meet the woman that he had dreamed and prayed for his entire life, he was not about to miss out on what was destined.

"Candice, are you sure I do not have anymore meetings planned?" Rebeccah asked while walking around her office as if she had misplaced something.

"Yes ma'am it's an empty schedule," she said while standing in the office door trying to figure out what her boss was looking for.

"Something is not right," Rebeccah stated looking at Candice.

"No ma'am. You have taken care of all of your business today. Pretty much you are ahead of schedule until next Monday."

"Next Monday! What about the quarterlies?"

"They are complete."

"And the new artist contracts?"

"Complete."

"My...."

"Everything is done that you had us set out to do for the week."

"The entire week?"

"Yes. See here in the books here," she said walking towards Rebeccah with the schedule.

"Hhm, I guess so. I must not be doing my job. I should have more things to do than that I know. What are my numbers looking like and the ratings?"

"All where you projected them to be."

"And I don't have a demo to do?"

"No ma'am. No vocals what-so-ever."

"For some reason this is hard for me to believe. But I guess we have been working extra hard these past few weeks. I like to keep busy," she said while thinking how she liked to keep herself occupied and not sit in the office doing nothing. "Well, if everything is empty than maybe I should go shopping or to the salon or something. I am in need of pampering myself. Call the salon and make an appointment for me."

"Yes ma'am," Candice said being hesitant.

"What's wrong, girl? Is everything fine? You seem disappointed. Don't worry. I will give you the rest of the day with full pay. You can go home or enjoy yourself. Go out have a good time."

"Not a problem. It's just..."

"What's that, Candi? You feel you need to work?"

"Oh-no! Not that at all."

For a minute Rebeccah thought Candice had been a little stressed because they *had* been working pretty hard and Candice did stay for the long haul, regardless of what time of day it was.

"Baby here is an advance," she said while going through her wallet and giving Candice whatever she had in the wallet; which happened to be six hundred dollars. "Just take the entire weekend off and enjoy yourself."

"Yes ma'am," she said smiling.

"And if you can call the salon as soon as possible to set up the appointment, I am going to shut down everything in here."

"Okay, will do boss."

Candice worried Rebeccah sometimes. She knew she was working her hard and that maybe she would let Candice off the hook for a few days. "Note to self, send Candice home early next late night."

A knock startled her while she put her pen down. She figured Candice was back with some good news or that she may have forgotten something.

"Come in. Were you able to make the appointment? I am so in need of some relaxation today, girl," she said looking at her desk and straightening up the last of the paperwork.

"Well I think I can assist you with that Ms. Carpenter," a deep voice said that sort of startled her.

"Oh my goodness, Brian! What are you doing here?"

"Here to whisk you away."

"What do you mean?"

"I mean I am here to take you on a surprise, something that I know will make you relax."

"Really now?" Rebeccah wasn't expecting Brian to be at her office. She figured Candice again was the culprit of changing her schedule. Any other time she would have fired her for not listening to her about making changes with the schedule. However, this was an exception. Rebeccah was happy to see Brian. She was learning so much from him and was grateful for the change that she was seeing within herself. Her friends and employees had noticed the difference in her, too. They said things like she was happier and calm compared to the way she used to be. It had only been a week since she and Brian had been talking, but a week to her could change things; especially after experiencing what she had been feeling when she was around him.

"I guess I can take the time for a surprise seeing that my schedule is clear," she said walking out of her office and glancing at Candice who was looking away when they made eye contact.

"Great Ms. Carpenter, let me get the door for you," he said winking at Candice as to say thank you.

"Candice, you can go home after you finish what you are doing and take the day yourself at the spa. But I will definitely see you in here on Saturday to do some last minute work before next week," Rebeccah said knowing that there was still some unfinished work that needed to be done in the office. After she put everything together she figured Candice had showed her a different calendar.

"Yes ma'am."

"By the way…"

"Yes ma'am," she said seeming a little nervous of what was about to come from Rebeccah's mouth.

"Thank you."

"You're welcome," she replied smiling relived that Rebeccah didn't fire her.

"Where are we going, Mr. Foster?"

"Oh so now you know how it feels, huh?"

"What do you mean, *now*?"

"I take it you don't like getting surprises do you?"

"You can say that. Most surprise parties I had I ended up throwing myself because I wanted to make sure everything would turn out right. *What*? What's with that look you're giving me right now?"

"Nothing. I hope you still aren't that way."

"No, I'm not."

"Good because I want you to enjoy the rest of the day, instead of being in control."

"Quiet as it's kept, I was already enjoying the rest of my day."

"So am I," he said while he held her hand stepping into the elevator.

Everything on the drive to the picnic was perfect.

There weren't any rain clouds in the sky with just the right amount of heat and sun. Simply put, it was a southern comfort day. Brian found the right spot for them to have their lunch. He had scouted out the area the day before and it felt, in his heart, like the right spot for him to ask her his major question that would alter both of their lives forever. He felt the Lord was completely on his side and he knew not to ever doubt the Almighty's powers.

Brian had Rebeccah put on a blindfold while they were in the car so that she wouldn't have a clue as to where they were going. He wanted everything to be a complete surprise; just as she had surprised him a few weeks earlier.

"Brian, why are you being so secretive right now?"

"Now that the tables are turned, you can't handle it can you?" he chuckled looking at the woman that the Lord had brought into his life and made him happy every chance he heard her name or saw her face.

"Maybe," she said turning her head in his direction unable to see due to her being blindfolded.

"I think you can't."

"Can I get some sort of clue?"

"Remember what you told me the night you flew me out to LA?"

"I told you a lot of things," she said sarcastically.

"That's questionable."

"I remember that I told you a few things about myself," she said trying to remember exactly what her words to him could have been.

"No, this wasn't about what you said about yourself, but what you told me when I kept asking you where we were going."

"Oh, *that* something that I told you."

"Right *that* something. If you want me to turn around and take you back to the office I can…"

"Nope, not at all. From this moment on my lips are

sealed," she said as if to zip her lips closed.

"Cool. Do you know that this is a lovely day," he said while looking at Rebeccah who just happened to be sitting there smiling. "I have been planning this for a minute now and I hope you enjoy it."

He looked over at Rebeccah again to see why she was not responding to him. There she was sitting silently grinning from ear to ear wanting to respond but something was holding her back.

"Why aren't you saying anything" he asked quizzically while she raised her hand like a child in Sunday school. He laughed, "Yes Rebeccah?"

"May I speak now?"

"Yes you may, Reebie," he loved the way her nickname sounded to him. He loved everything about her.

"Good, cause I wanted to talk."

"I didn't tell you not to. *You* said that your lips were sealed."

"Okay you got me," as they both, laughed.

He realized that he had never felt so at ease and happy before as he was with her in his life. He had no worries to think of just that he was happy living in the moment and being in the presence of Gods beauty.

"Why are you so silent?"

"I'm just thinking," Rebeccah said.

"Thinking about what?"

"Thinking about how wonderful it is to relax. You know for some reason my senses seem to be open; maybe because you shut off one of them with this blindfold. Can I take it off?" she asked while trying to take it off.

"No you may not take it off. It will ruin the surprise. You are a hard one to deal with I can see."

"I am not."

"Its okay. I enjoy it anyway. You still over there smiling?"

"Yes, because I'm happy."

He understood what she meant. Brian was completely at peace with himself and her being present. Work was left behind while they kept driving forward to their destination. Every problem with church, even nosey Lesha, seemed to disappear as their journey down the road to what seemed like heaven, was soothing.

"We are almost here but when I get out of the car I want you to stay seated for at least a few minutes."

"Okay. Are you going to leave me here?"

"No, I'm not. I just need a few minutes to do something and whatever you do, please do not touch the scarf."

"Okay I promise. I wont."

"Good 'cause I trust you."

As he parked the car near the grass and trees, he couldn't help but thank God for allowing the day to be so beautiful.

"Reebie,"

"Yes," she said while turning her head towards his voice.

Brian wanted to tell her that he was falling for her but he didn't know how to form the right words nor could they come out. The only thing he could bring his mouth to say was, "you are so beautiful."

"Thank you," she grinned looking innocent and embarrassed at the same time.

"I will be right back. Just give me a few seconds. "Just a few, okay?"

"Okay. I will be here waiting with bells on."

Brian was getting nervous with each step while getting ready to set up. He didn't want her to see how nervous he was, which is why he was thankful that still had her blindfold on. He knew that everything had to be just right as he glanced at her in the car. He opened the back passenger door and took the basket out praying that she would enjoy what he cooked; especially since he worked on it for what seemed like hours trying to get the chicken breaded just right. Brian walked a little bit away from the car to a spot that was not in full sun and opened up the basket. He freaked out for a minute but then remembered that he had put the blanket in the trunk earlier. He ran back to the car and opened the front door to check on Rebeccah.

"Are you still okay in here?"

"I'm fine."

"You aren't peaking are you?"

"No, I'm being a good girl."

"Good. Give me a few more seconds."

"I'll be here waiting."

Brian slowly closed her door and went to his trunk to open it. He pulled out the blanket and his Bible. They had been doing a lot of studying together lately so he had to be prepared. He closed the trunk and hurried back to where he left the basket. The turquoise blanket was nice and plush. He even had a few throw pillows which were made from the same material; just to make it a little more comfortable while at their picnic. Brian had bet that Mama Jenkins sewed everything for his special occasion. He knew that she was good with her hands. He set out the food and plates wanting to make an impression on Rebeccah since she did the same for him.

"Lord, I hope everything will taste the way she likes it," he mumbled to himself as he ran back to the car almost tripping over a root from a big oak tree. Brian looked around hoping Rebeccah did not notice him and his misstep. She was still sitting there contently as he opened her door for a second time.

"Are you ready?" he asked while he looked at her with ease.

"Ready as I will ever be," she smiled

"Grab my hand and trust me to guide you."

She did just that and he made sure she knew not to trip over the same root sticking out of the ground that he previously tripped over. Finally they made it to the edge of the blanket.

"I'm about to take the blindfold off. You ready?"

"I think I am. Are we near some water?"

"*Maybe*. You'll see in just a second. Keep your eyes closed when I take this off, ok?"

"Okay."

He didn't realize how much they were close in height. He didn't want to get too close to her because he new his ordained self had to obey everything that was not of flesh; although it was hard for him. He did however keep his composure because he knew that she was more than just any woman. She was the woman of his dreams.

"Your eyes closed?" he asked again while untying the scarf.

"Yes."

Brian took the blindfold from around her head and told her to open her eyes. She looked around realizing where she was and then looked down.

"Oh my God Brian, you did all of this?"

"Yes with a little help, but yes I did."

"How did you know that I liked coming out here and relaxing? How did you know that this is my favorite tree in this park? How did you know?"

"So you like it?" he asked pleased with his choices.

"Yes I like it! More than like it." She turned to him and gave him a hug.

"It was nice to be held again; to be loved and accepted, for the first time not being a man held captive by his past, but one of the present," he thought to himself.

She almost cried when she had seen where Brian had taken her. This was the place Rebeccah would come when everything else seemed to stress her out. The location was beautiful with a stream that ran into a large lake that had swans and ducks swimming in it. She knew that this was the untouched part of the park and had flowing trails that anyone hardly ever walked. She was at peace.

"Have a seat," Brian said while helping her sit down.

"Brian, this is wonderful."

"I was hoping you would like it," he nervously smiled while sitting down next to her. "This was my way of thanking you for being such an inspiration and good friend."

"You're greatly welcome and thank you."

"Before we eat, I wanted to say a prayer," Brian grabbed both of her hands and began to pray.

While he was praying, she could tell that he seemed a little nervous. His palms were sweaty and hands trembling. She knew that she should have been praying as well and paying attention to the prayer, but all she kept thinking about was how wonderful the Lord truly was for bringing someone like Brian into her life. He calmed her down and taught her a lot about the Lord in the past few weeks. She was beginning to grow in Christ with the help of Brian. It was as if he completed her.

"Amen."

"Amen," Rebeccah followed knowing that she was not quite listening and hoped the Lord had forgiven her for being somewhere else in her mind. She was content.

"I hope you like what is on our menu for today," Brian said while handing her a blue and cream paper that read *Today's Menu.*

"Brian, these are my favorite things. How did you know?"

"A few angels helped me."

That Candice, Rebeccah thought to herself and wondered what she was going to do with her. Candice was completely helpful but she also was overly helpful. Rebeccah didn't mind at the moment because she was finally happy being with someone who made her feel at ease.

"Yes, I guess we all have a few angels in our lives," she said looking at Brian and then at what he brought out of the basket. "Chicken Parmesan, hmm this sure does smell good. The salad looks wonderful, too."

"I hope you like it. I'll bring out dessert a little later."

As they sat there and had lunch, the idea of her being married to Brian didn't matter one bit. She knew marriage was way out there as an idea however, it did cross her mind. *We hadn't even gone through the courtship process or thing- a- ma-bob that he had talked to her about* she thought while enjoying the moment. She surmised it was still too early in their relationship for them to go through it. Little did she know what Brian had planned.

"Brian, everything tastes delicious. How come you are barely eating?"

"I just have a lot on my mind. I wanted this to be just right for you, especially since you showed me a wonderful time in LA. It's not like I had that kind of money to go to the extravagant but, I wanted to do something special for you."

"Brian, it has nothing to do with money at all with me. It honestly and truly is the thought that counts. Trust me, no one with money has ever gone this far as to say thank you to me."

"That's hard to believe."

"Is it really?"

"Yeah, a little," he paused and then looked into her eyes. "Reebie, you are so genuine and nice I don't see why anyone would never do anything for you. You have a good spirit."

"You know people in my business are only nice for one reason, to get something out of you. If you've noticed the only true friends that I have are Kathy and Terry, and that's because I have known them for some time now. Other than that, industry people I can never say are my true friends."

"It must be a hard life for you, especially being a woman in a male driven industry."

"To a point, it is. I have built up a good reputable business so no man, or woman, can say that my work is shabby. Trust. I had to fight to get to where I am now, but in the end, I think it's worth it."

"Is it really worth it. Are you really happy?"

"Why I like you because you can see through all of the stuff and see what is really bothering me."

"I see you because I am a lot like you."

"And how is that?"

"I have to watch people just like you do. Just because some folks go to church doesn't mean that they are upstanding citizens in society. The drama they have at home, or on the job, they bring to church with them. There are also those who want me to see them and acknowledge every little thing that they do. In the end, I am not the one that they should be impressing. I also have the drama starters because of my age. It's just like any other business; a lot of older people feel that I cannot lead them. 'How can he tell me what to do when my children are his age, he's just a child.' In reality I am, but I have had this calling on me for some time now."

"I didn't know you had it so hard."

"It gets worse, but there will be time for those stories later. I want this afternoon to be about us if you don't mind."

"Sure, I don't mind at all. Can I ask you something though? You don't have to answer if you feel that I am prying too much into your business."

"Sure go ahead."

"What made you decide that this is what you wanted to do be, I mean being a preacher? You are a little younger than most preachers that I have seen."

"Reebie, being called by the Lord has nothing to do with what I choose or decide. There comes a time in a persons life when they beat themselves up for not listening and follow the Lords will instead of stopping and doing it. Let me see, how can I explain it? When your parent tells you to clean your room or wash the dishes as a child, what do you tend to do?"

"Get mad, act like I don't hear, or better yet go outside and play."

"But there are consequences to that, right?"

"True."

"When you come back inside and those dishes still aren't washed, you get the beat down of your life. Right or wrong?"

"Right," she said grinning.

"Well, that's the same as with dealing with the Lord when he says you need to preach my child; especially when He has given me all the tools to work with and if I don't do it then...."

"You get the beat down of your life."

"Exactly!... I never noticed that."

"Noticed what?"

"The way your eyes light up when you are happy and that dimple right there on your cheek," he said while pointing to it. "That's so cute."

"Stop! You're making me blush."

"It's ok. When you see beauty you should acknowledge it, it's like thanking God for what He has created."

Brian made her blush even more and she couldn't help but smile even harder which made her dimple appear even stronger.

"There it is again! I like that."

"Your making me blush. Stop," she said coyly.

"Ok I'll stop. Okay maybe not."

She gave him a stern look and he started laughing with her even more.

"Is that how you plan on being when you have children?" he asked.

"How's that?" she asked unaware of what he meant.

"Smiling at them all the time with that cute dimple? They won't believe anything you say."

"Yes they will. I'll be like, 'sit yo'self down, boy! Didn't I tell you to do those dishes,'" she said in her stern mother voice and pointing in the air as if to scold a child but all she could do was laugh.

"See, that won't work at all," he said laughing and then admired her beauty once again. "You're beautiful, Rebeccah."

"You're not so bad yourself, Brian," she shyly replied. She then had to look away because she didn't want to tempt the man in any way. She needed to be on her best behavior. She wasn't sure why, but she knew she didn't need to be the forward Rebeccah who got what she wanted when she wanted it. Instead, she was learning and evolving into someone who was much more.

"I'll take your plate." He said while reaching out to take it.

"Thank you," she said turning around again to look at Brian.

"You're welcome," he replied softly. He took the plate out of her hand, picked up his, and placed it alongside the basket. Then he reached in the basket taking out two glasses of her all time favorite, chocolate mousse.

"You did not make this did you?"

"Of course I did," he grinned handing her a glass with a spoon. "Here you go."

"This looks all fancy like in the restaurants. You even have shaved chocolate on top. Are you sure you made this?"

"Yes I am sure I made it, silly woman."

"Oh my goodness this taste so delicious and it's rich and creamy with a hint of espresso. Oh my gosh, this is heavenly. Boy you outdid yourself," she said looking directly at Brian while taking another spoonful of the mousse.

"I'm glad you like it."

"Do you always cook?"

"I try too but since everyone knows that I am single, the women at the church bring me plates just about everyday."

"Do you eat a lot of it?"

"Not always. *Some* women can not cook like they say they can," he said shaking his head while making a bitter face.

"I hope the breakfast I made for you that day was great."

"It was more than great," he grinned taking a spoonful of mousse.

"How often do women approach you?"

"Do you really want to know?" he asked while looking into her eyes.

"Yeah, I really want to know," she said with curiosity in her voice.

"Every chance they get."

"Are you serious?" she shockingly asked.

"Yes I am serious. Sometimes its sad seeing women go to the extremes that they do in order to get my attention."

"Is it *that* bad?"

"Yes it's that bad."

"Nuh-uh not in the church," she said a little baffled.

"Yes in the church. I told you, most folk are not completely who they say they are."

"Well let me ask you this then."

"Ok. Shoot."

"Did I tell you this is good by the way?"

"Yes you did. And thank you," he smiled while wiping off some chocolate from her chin with his handkerchief.

"Welcome," she said getting the last bit she had out of the glass scraping the sides before she finally realized what she was doing. "Boy I am so sorry but this was good. I hope I don't appear to be too greedy."

"Not at all, you just know what you want and what you like. I am thankful that you liked it," he said reaching his hand out for the glass. "I'll take that for you."

"Thank you. That was good," she said finally putting the empty glass down but still holding the spoon in her hand. "Next time we meet up I would like some more of that, please."

"Next time?"

"Yes, next time! I'm sure we aren't finished seeing one another, especially with the revival coming up. You'll have a little more time to visit me I hope."

"If I don't, I will make time."

"Ok. Now back to what I was saying. I get sidetracked sometimes. Sorry about that but I wanted to ask you this. You told me your definition of love before, but what kind of woman do *you* want to share your love with?"

"Strange that you should ask me that. I have been thinking about that for a couple of days now and a few things come to mind."

"Oh yeah. Like what?"

"For starters, I want to make sure I can trust the woman completely," he said while handing Rebeccah a wet whip.

"Thank you."

"You're welcome," he said while getting comfortable on his pillow. "And second, she has to be very courteous."

"But what about looks?" Rebeccah curiously asked.

"Don't get me wrong, looks are always important, but they are not the main thing that holds together a relationship. There has to be a little attraction to at least wake up your senses in recognizing who you need in your life."

"What about lifestyle?"

"Lifestyle has to be pleasing to God, no street walker or haughty woman will suffice."

"Does she have to be a church going woman?"

"If at first she isn't, that's fine but, eventually it would be nice that she were being that I am a Preacher."

"What if the woman was doubtful of things?"

"Things like what?" he asked unsure of her question then looking up, "About the Lord?"

"No not that. But doubtful about changing her lifestyle; having to give it all up kind of doubtful."

"She would have to ask herself why is she afraid to give up what she is familiar with in order to move forward with what is planned for her. Is this woman afraid of change?"

"I don't know. I am just saying if you were to come across a woman like that," she said trying not to make it obvious that the woman that she was referring to was herself.

"If I were to come across a woman like that, I would hold her hand, look into her eyes and say to her that everything would be fine and that I would never let her fall or steer her in the wrong direction," he said while turning her head towards his and holding her hand.

They sat there for what seemed like eternity. She felt as if they were lost in each others eyes until Brian's cell phone rang.

"You're an interesting man, you know that," as she had waken up from her admiration of Brian. "Aren't you going to answer your phone?"

"Nah, it's no one important," he said without even glancing at it. "I'm going to turn off my phone."

Ok this man is the most perfect man I have been with and have understood in my entire life. I really enjoy him completely, Rebeccah thought to herself.

Mike had almost ruined the mood that Brian and Rebeccah were in. Brian knew it was him by the ringtone. Right when his cell phone had rang, Brian was about to ask Rebeccah if she was interested in wanting to date him. He knew that what Mike wanted was not important. It was a Thursday afternoon and Mike wanted to go to a basketball game later, but Brian was happy right where he was; with Rebeccah.

"Is everything okay?" Rebeccah asked a little concerned.

"Yes, just fine. Now where were we," he said as he turned off his cell phone.

"Sitting here admiring life," she replied.

"That's right, admiring life," he paused. "Since you were asking some questions, do you mind if I ask you a few?"

"Sure, go right ahead," she chirped.

"Where do you see yourself in five years?"

"Business wise, or family?"

"Both."

"Good question," she responded while gathering her thoughts. "In five years business wise, I'm not sure. Things have been changing for me lately and I am still considering selling the company?"

"Have you ever thought about doing Gospel music?"

"It still crosses my mind from time to time."

"It would be nice seeing us both work for the Lord you know."

"Are you recruiting me or something?"

"No. I'm just saying it would be nice," he said without giving away what was on his mind. "What about family? Where do you see yourself with that?"

"I haven't really thought about having a family. I always put it on the back burner and think that if it is meant to be, then I would actually enjoy being a mother and wife."

"Really?"

"Yeah!"

"I could see you making a wonderful wife, and mother," he said grinning.

"You think?"

"Yes, of course. If you ran your household like you run your business, you would make the Lord, your husband, and family proud."

"I never compared the Lord and a family in anything that I did."

"The Lord is in everything that we do. From the smallest job of picking up cans on the side of the road, to being a record label owner who can travel across the globe and speak four different languages."

"I guess so when you put it that way. And it's *five* languages Mr." she corrected him.

"I know. I just wanted to see if you would correct me with your ghetto slang."

"You are so silly," she smiled.

"Rebeccah, you asked me in honesty what I look for in a woman."

"Yes, that I did."

"I want you to read something," he said as he sat up while reaching in the basket. "Let me get my Bible."

He handed her a turquoise box with a cream ribbon around it while also grabbing his Bible.

"What is this, Brian?"

"*Well*, you have to open it to see what's inside," he said trying to cover up being nervous.

Rebeccah pulled the ribbon slowly as if the contents of the package were fragile. She then opened the lid to find a blue envelope.

"What is this, Brian," Rebeccah replied.

"Just open it, open it," he said worried that she may not enjoy the gift that he had gotten her.

She opened up the envelope and read the note to

herself.

> *To the woman in my life that I have found to be virtuous. Turn to Proverbs 31:10*
>
> *Brian*

"What does this mean," she asked while looking at the note and in the box for more information. When she looked up, Brian had another box in his hand.

"Brian, what have you done? You have outdone yourself. What's in this one?" she asked while pointing at the new package.

"You have to open it. I am not telling you," he looked a little nervous again afraid of what she might say and handed her the gift.

She hesitated for a second, "Brian!"

"What? Here is the second gift. I hope you like it."

The next gift that he had given her was the same color as the last but a little heavier. She opened up the gift afraid of what she would find until she noticed another card in a cream envelope that read:

> *This card leads you to Proverbs 31:10.*
>
> *Brian*

She un-wrapped the tissue from around the gift which happened to be her own Bible with her name on the cover in cream writing. It had a turquoise suede cover and dividers on each chapter. The Bible also had a concordance with both the NIV and King James versions. She turned to the first page and it read:

> *Thank you for being such a dear and lovely friend with complete and utter love and blessings.*
>
> *Brian*

"This is just like yours, huh?" she asked with a slight tear in her eye.

"Yes, but what did the card ask for you to do?"

"It said to read Proverbs 31:10," she said while she turned her new Bible to Proverbs 31 to find one more envelope. She slowly opened it up and it said:

Rebeccah, you are to me the Virtuous woman that I have been looking for and need in my life.

Rebeccah looked up at Brian who was now leaning behind her with another box in his hand that he opened for her. He pulled out a necklace that had a cross made of diamonds and platinum with a turquoise blue stone in the center. He placed it around her neck as she pulled her hair to the side. She felt as if she were in heaven.

"Brian, this is nice," she said while tears began to roll down her cheek. "Thank you."

"No, Reebie, thank you," he said while clasping the necklace.

She could tell that he was still a little nervous so she touched his hand to calm him.

He sat down next to her and said, "Thank you for being here at this moment in time and for being here to show me that I waited for the right reason at the right time. I wanted to know if you would be my girlfriend."

"After all of this," she cried, "who could say no? Yes Brian, yes I will be your girlfriend."

With that, he gave her a kiss on her cheek, said a prayer, and they set in the park holding each others hands under her favorite oak tree, by her favorite stream, where the swans and ducks swam, surrounded by nothing but the Lord.

Chapter
10

To everything there is a season, and a time to every purpose under heaven...

"This is what I need you to do for me. I don't trust this lady and she is getting in the way of me and my man," a mysterious female voice said over the phone.

"Oh, no doubt! He thinks he's all better than everyone else. He acts like he does not know where he came from," an angry man replied.

"Look, look. I just want you to handle it, ok?"

"I got you little momma, don't even trip. Normally I wouldn't do this but all of this changing has got to stop," he reiterated.

"Whatever! I owe you one. Just do this for me and I will pay you big later. You know I got the money."

"Fa sho."

Rebeccah sat at her desk thinking about her day at the park with Brian. She knew that there were times when she was close to something that she needed in her life.

Normally that would be the case in her business venture, but this time it was in love. Regardless of how hard she would try to act, regardless of who she was and what she did, Brian still liked her. She felt that he had really found her match. He actually wanted to know her for who she was and he accepted everything that she was about without having to change her. She contemplated on giving up her lifestyle in order to be with a preacher. It was still something that she was not sure she could do. Brian hadn't asked her to marry him but they were hitting it off lately. Her thoughts begin to drift to her meeting with him later on that evening and how it would be when she left the office.

Rebeccah was bombarded with last minute work that needed to do before her quarter releases. She sent everyone home since all of their work was done. Candice wanted to stay but she let her leave a few minutes before hand. Rebeccah yearned to leave seeing that the only thing or person she could think about was Brian and getting anything accomplished was a hard task. She knew that his past had been tainted, but whose hasn't. However, she didn't mind because what he currently helped those who he could have possibly hurt if he were still in the streets. Brian had even taught her that people can change, regardless of what goes wrong. He had influenced her so much, that she found herself even quoting scriptures from the Bible.

Rebeccah had surprised herself about knowing and learning more about the Lord each day. She noticed that she was growing in Christ and craved to learn more. Brian had brought her through so many things and she was very thankful now that she had come to know the Lord in a better light. She was changing, even to the point that it didn't matter if she were to be married to a man of the cloth. Being a woman working for the Lord was something that she could see herself doing in the near future.

"Excuse me," a deep masculine voice said while standing at her office door. "Are you Ms. Carpenter?"

"Oh! you scared me," she jumped a little. "I didn't know they left the front door unlocked."

"I just let myself in."

"And how may I help you this evening," she asked trying not to seem nervous. She looked around her desk for her cell phone and then her mace because she felt something about this stranger did not feel right.

"That's a good question," he said while walking towards her. "How may you help me?"

"Do I know you?" she asked while standing up trying to see if she could make a run for the door. He was right between her and the exit.

"I can't say that you do, or you don't," he sarcastically remarked. "But what I do know is that you are a single woman in this little office all by yourself this late in the evening."

"Excuse me but I don't think you need to be here," she said angrily.

"Calm down, Ms. Lady. You shouldn't fear me," he said moving in closer to her.

"Not trying to be rude or anything but can you come back at a better time," she tried reaching for something sharp on her desk without him noticing. "I have so much that I have to do and I am not able to talk right now."

"You know what, you are right you don't need to talk right now," he said while pushing her towards her desk. "All you need to do is do what I say."

"Oh my God! I am going to scream!"

"Scream all you want baby because no one will be able to hear you," he said while starting to rub on her arms.

"No stop," she said trying to push him away from her. "Stop!"

"Now you want to act all timid and everything," he

said while he started to tear off her clothes.

"No," she started crying, "stop!"

"Shut up you low down dirty bitch," he said slapping her.

"Don't, please don't."

"I thought I just told you to shut up, bitch," he reached behind his back while putting a gun to her head. "This will make you shut up."

"*God no, no. Don't let this man kill me. No,*" she cried to herself.

"Yeah, now you gonna listen and listen good. You have come into Brian's life and taken him away from me and the life he once knew. No longer will he want you. See, this is my world and now since you have taken away what was mine, you gotta pay. You hear me, you gone pay bitch!"

With that Mike did what any evil man would do. He took her dignity. She felt that maybe she deserved what was happening to her, that maybe she was not destined to have someone and something special in her life.

God why is this happening to me? Why are you letting this man do this to me? God, just let this pain stop, let him stop.

"Oh my God! What happened here?" Rebeccah could hear Candice screaming in the background. Oh no, Beccah, what happened? Who did this to you? Hello 9-1-1. I need you to get here right away! My boss has been raped. There is blood everywhere. Please hurry! I don't know the address right now. Don't you have it on your caller id? Look, just get here send the cops, the ambulance, something, somebody! She's bleeding to death! It's gonna be ok Ms. Carpenter, you're gonna be ok. Hurry up, she's passing out!"

"Ms. Carpenter you are going to be ok. We have the police officers outside if...."

"I don't want to talk to them right now. I just want to rest. Can you tell them to leave!"

"But it's important if you talk to them right now."

"I *said* I don't want to see them, I want them to leave!"

"Ok, if you say so," the nurse said in disagreement.

"Yes I do please," Rebeccah replied while lying in a fetal position on the hospital bed. She was filled with so much pain, her head was throbbing, and she was confused.

She didn't know why any of what happened at her office happened to her. She could still smell the man that had hurt her and she wanted to wash his scent off of her. She was angry.

"Reebie!" Terry said running into her hospital room. "Oh baby, are you ok?"

"I'm ok," she lied.

"Who did this to you, babygirl?" he angrily said trying not to let her see him cry.

"Please, Terrance! I don't feel like talking about it right now."

"I understand. If you need anything right now I do not mind doing it for you."

"I just want to be left alone!"

"Now that is something I am not going to do," he sternly replied. "I am going to be by your side as long as you need me here."

"Don't you have the revival tomorrow?"

"That can wait. You are more important to me at this

moment then a church reunion."

"I guess you know I will not be able to sing for you," she sadly said while also feeling guilty.

"Baby, *that* is the furthest thing from my mind right now, seriously," Terry said while wanting to console his friend the best way that he knew how.

"You know, Terry. I try my best to do right. I have been going to church now for a while, and was learning as much as I could. But for the life of me, how in the world can God allow something so wrong happen to a person. I mean I called for Him I asked for help and nothing happened to stop this man, evil man, from doing this to me.

What is it that I have done wrong? Have I hurt someone in the past? I know Karma comes back to haunt you, but never in my life I feel I have hurt someone *this* bad," she cried looking for answers.

"You know, Reebie, God does things everyday that we cannot understand while we are going through it. In the end, there is a lesson that we must learn."

"And what lesson would that be! Aside from my being stupid and sitting in the office that late by myself is the only thing that I can think of. I do it all the time why now, what is it in my character that has allowed me to be manipulated and taken advantage of? I just, I just try so hard to do right by others and now look at me I am a mess. I feel horrible, I......."

"It's ok, Reebie," Terry said while his friend cried on his shoulder. "Let it all out. Just don't blame yourself for any of this. Some things, heck all things in life we do not have control over. We do however have choices that we make, but control over our own lives we cannot do. All things we go through are test. We may not like them, but they are test. This may be hard for you to believe but right now your journey may be to show God that you are truly faithful to Him, that you truly adore Him for who He is."

"But how can I adore someone who I cannot see and am I am angry at?"

"Reebie, I know this is hard and like I say, this is going to take time for you. Of course, to you, God may not be visible in the way you see me or yourself, not at all times. The Lord is around you everyday, be it the smallest ant that crawls on the grown working hard, to the tall mountains planted on this earth that protect us from storms. The Lord even uses people during certain times, for a second, if you pay attention to the details. The Lord is in the details."

For a moment Terry's words soothed Rebeccah when she thought about how meticulous she could be when it came to her work. All the finite details have to be just right for her and it showed. She imagined that the Lord was the same way. All small things were just as important as the bigger picture. Of course, Rebeccah still felt she needed a prayer to help move her forward and to help stop the anger and neglect that she had been feeling.

"Terry?"

"Yes, babygirl."

"Can I ask you something?" as she began to cry again.

"Sure, what is it love?" he asked while holding his closest friend next to him without hurting her.

"Would I be asking too much from God if I asked you to pray for me right now?"

"It is never too much for the Lord when you come to Him in prayer, especially when you are humbled amongst His presence. I am definitely honored to pray for you and with you."

"Say girl, you doin' ok?" Kathy said while stepping into the room.

"You came just in time," Terry said while grabbing Katy's hand. "We are about to do some serious praying for, and with, our Sister in Christ."

With that, both Terry and Kathy held Rebeccah and

prayed. She felt the true detail in the moment was not what had happened to her earlier in her office, but who found her and when she was there in just the nick of time, and who was praying for her and with her. *To God be all the Glory in the midst of a storm!*

Chapter
11

A time to be born and a time to die...

"Good morning, Brian," Lesha said with a slight smirk walking into his study.

Here we go once again he thought because he was not ready to see her. He did notice that at least she was dressed a little more presentable. "Good morning sister," he replied.

"I hope you don't mind my coming in here before service starts this morning."

"No, not at all," he said looking over his sermon. "My door is always open to members."

"I just wanted to say that whatever you need me to do, any singing today, I would be honored."

"Well, you know sister that is not my department. My job is to help bring souls closer to God. Brother Hunt is the one that will handle that. You may need to speak with him, but I am sure it is a little late for any last minute additions."

"I'm not sure if he will be here today since he has some important business he needs to take care of," she smartly replied.

"Brother Hunt not coming to church," he said finally looking up. "Are you sure about that?"

"I just figured since, oh never mind. Just in case if he

doesn't make it, I do not mind helping you in that process at all," she said while giving him a wink.

"Well, I appreciate your help," he responded looking back over his notes.

"Not a problem at all," she retorted. "If you need anything, anything at all I will be here for you all day."

"Thank you again, sister. I need to get back to my sermon before service starts," he said trying not to sound irritated.

"Ok see you, honey," she said walking out of his door and looking back to see if he noticed the way she was walking out of his office.

Brian felt that something was not right with her at all. The comment she made about Brother Hunt not making it in disturbed him. He knew that Brother Hunt not showing up was something out of the ordinary. If it were an issue, Terrence would have called the church if anything out of the ordinary would come up. Brian needed him today because he knew that he was a major player on the Lord's team.

"Excuse me, Pastor," Mama Jenkins said while tapping on his door, "someone is here to see you."

"Ok, Sister Jenkins. Send them in," he said noticing how nice Mama Jenkins looked. "Oh hello, Candice. How are you?"

"I could be better, much better," she said looking a little disturbed.

"How is the Junior Class coming along?"

"Just great! Uhm, uhm. Well can I talk to you for a minute?"

"Sure what seems to be the problem," he stood up pulling out a chair for her to sit in. He noticed that she had been crying. "Is one of your students for Christ acting up?"

"Oh it's not that at all. I mean, I know this is none of my business and all but," she said fidgeting with the handkerchief she had in her hand.

"Please have a seat."

"Thank you, but I… How do I put this? I know that you are talking to Ms. Carpenter and it really isn't supposed to be any of my business but…"

"What's wrong," he noticed the worried look on her face.

"Well, last night I went to the office because I had forgotten to send out some files, and when I got there I saw Ms. Collins lying on the floor covered in blood," she began to cry.

"Oh my God, she what?" he was really worried and wanted, needed, to know more.

"Right now she is at Cedar Mercy Hospital in room 246. She is doing much better but I wanted to tell you first. I'm not sure if Brother Hunt will be here because the last I talked to him, he was still at the hospital."

"Is she doing fine? Is everything ok? What happened to her?"

"She is fine, all things considering. If I didn't show up when I did she, she…" she began crying even harder.

"Listen, did she tell you what had happened?"

"No," she sniffed. "She was unconscious when I found her last night. I stayed at the hospital as long as I possibly could until I informed her family. I didn't want to leave her again. For some reason I feel like part of this is my fault."

"No, you shouldn't say that," he said trying to console her.

"No, I should. I could have stayed late with her but instead, I was in the wrong for leaving her," Candice cried.

"What you can do for her now is pray that things will be better for you and her, sister." Brian wanted so bad to leave the church and go to the hospital to check on Rebeccah but by then Brother Hunt walked into the office.

"Is everything ok Brother Hunt?" Brian asked

worriedly.

"Not as good as we would like it to be," Terry said looking at both Brian and Candace. "Rebeccah is fine but she will not be able to make it to church today. She was released this morning from the hospital, but I don't feel she wants to be bothered today. One thing she did say was that she wanted you to call her."

"Brother Foster, your class is ready," Sister Jenkins said while tapping on the door.

"Excuse me just a second," Brian said to them walking out into the hallway. "Uhm, excuse me Deacon Price. Can you start the class for me today? There are some things I need to take care of."

"Sure, Pastor. Is everything ok?"

"Yes sir, everything is fine," he said patting the Deacon on the back with a look of concern on his face.

"Ok, I'll take care of it for you," the Deacon replied.

"I guess I'll go and get my class ready, too," said Candice.

"You don't have to if you aren't ready," Brian said walking back into his office.

"No, that's fine. You are right. I need to keep God's work in mind. I'll be fine. Brother Hunt, let me know of any updates," she said while getting up to walk out of the office.

"I sure will, sister," Terry said giving Candice a hug. "If you need me for anything, just call me."

"Ok," she said walking out and closing the door behind her.

Brian's mind was on Rebeccah and wanted to know more about what had happened to her. He didn't know if he would be able to stand up before the church and preach because he was so worried about her. He asked the Lord to guide him and show him how to handle the day and to give him guidance for doing the right thing. Brian knew that the Lord had him at the church to do work at the Revival which was put upon his heart to do. *Lord, please be with me.*

"Is everything ok, Pastor," Terry asked.

"Yes, everything is fine. What exactly happened to Rebeccah?"

"She wouldn't say. The only thing she told me was that she wanted me to come to church and that she would be fine."

"Did she look okay?"

"Man, I wish I could say yes but I do not want to lie. Something has really spooked her. Kathy and I followed her home. She asked that Kathy stay with her and that I leave because she felt that 'the show had to go on.' Typical Reebie, still about business," he said trying to see the joy in what was hard to make out of such sorrow.

"Yes brother she is very head strong," Brian assured him.

"I love that woman, Pastor. She's like a sister to me. I just want to know who did this to her and why," he said a little angrily while tears began to build up in his eyes.

"Revenge is not the key. Forgiveness is what should be in your heart right now."

"But this is hard. And poor Candice finding her in her office on the floor. I can just imagine what is going through her mind."

"I know, I told her to pray on it."

"But Pastor, what do you do when you have so much anger in your heart and fear, how then are you able to pray?"

"You should never run on emotions, all that is the devil taking advantage of the situation and wanting to have control over your soul. If you are open to allow his thoughts into your spirit, he feels he has conquered God."

"You know you are right, but still I am just upset with all of this," he said while tears rolled down his face. "Even the fact that Reebie will not tell me exactly what is going on with her... I just don't know."

"Right now, this is not for us to know but to learn from. In the end, we can look back at this and know that there was a bigger plan. This is just a small test to see if we are really trusting in the Lord. She wanted you to come to church to still run the choir for the revival, right?"

"Yes," Terry said drying his eyes.

"Think about this, the Lord uses those in times of weakness. At her weakest point her spirit, vessel, was still open to whisper something so powerful. This revival still must go on and the Lord knows this. He used her when everyone around would listen."

"You are an amazing man, Pastor."

"This is not me at all. This is our Father who uses me just like He will use you. Pray on it and let's honor His will."

"That I will do and please call her, not just for her, but also for me. Maybe your words will encourage her as well."

Brian knew that Terry was thanking him in his own special way. He also wondered about what was the lesson that he needed to learn from the new information that had just been given to him about Rebeccah. *Lord what is your bigger plan? Please guide me.*

Rebeccah was feeling completely sore since she made it home from the hospital. She finally noticed herself in the mirror and did not like what she had seen. She had taken a shower over three times just to get the ugly off of her. She was not sure about what she was feeling but one thing she did know, she was afraid. The thought crossed her mind that maybe the guy that had done those things to her would show up again. She kept hearing him mention Brian's name over and over again in her head and wanted to know what kind of connection Brian had with him. She couldn't blame Brian. She wanted to blame herself.

"What have I done to deserve all of this," she yelled. "Why me, Lord? Why me?"

"Reebie, you ok in there," Kathy asked while standing at the bathroom door.

"Yes I'm fine," she said wiping the tears away. "I'll be out in just a second."

"Ok girl, call me if you need me," Kathy said sounding concerned for her friend.

"Thank you God for the friends you have sent into my life," she whispered to herself still standing in front of the bathroom mirror.

Rebeccah wanted to be at the revival, but she didn't want people looking at her in the state that she was in. She felt guilty and she figured everyone would spot it. She really felt filthy, as if she were the scum at the bottom of the earth. Rebeccah had sent Terry to church because she didn't want him to feel or be responsible for her. She knew he needed to work for the Lord. Terry's calling was more important, she felt, then being with her. She prayed that her ideology for thinking was not making her selfish, she just wanted the Lords will to be done.

"Reebie, sorry to bother you again," Kathy said.

Rebeccah almost jumped out of her skin when she heard the knock on the bathroom door. *Please Lord, guide me.*

"You have a phone call. It's Brian, I mean Pastor Foster." Kathy announced while correcting herself.

"Ok. Here I come girl, give me a second."

Rebeccah put her sweats and hooded shirt over her scared body, even though it was 100 degrees outside. She wanted to hide in her own personal shell. She asked Terry to have Brian call her when he saw him at church if he would be able to see him before services would start. She wasn't sure why she wanted him to call her but she felt the need to maybe hear his voice or to see if he knew the man that had taken her dignity away from her. The man did mention Brian's name. She slowly opened the bathroom door and peaked around the corners to see if anyone else was in her bedroom. *Lord why am I so paranoid? Will I have to live my life this way forever?* She picked up the phone that Kathy had laid on her bed. Katy had walked out earlier to give Rebeccah some space. She could hear her in the kitchen making something for them to eat. *Thank you God again for her.*

"Hello," she said afraid that he could see her condition over the phone.

"Hello, Miss Lady. Are you ok?" he asked softly.

"Yes I am fine, all things considered." She didn't know what to say to him but she wanted to say something. The tears began forming. *Lord where do I start? I know that I am still new to having you in my life and I am learning and growing each day, being closer to you. Lord I ask You to guide me so that I may be the person that I need to be for You and that I may say the right thing at this moment.* "I just, I just wanted to tell you that," she paused, "wow, this is real hard without crying."

"It's ok Rebeccah take your time. Matter of fact do you need me to come over?"

"No, no," she said shaking her head in fear of how he would judge her if he saw her. "Not right now. You have too many things that you must do today. It's your big day and I don't want to take you away from that."

"You won't take me away at all. Whenever you need me, I will be here to help."

"I know and I understand that, but that would be selfish of me. I know that you have something that you need to share with more than one today. You have an entire church to look over and guide. I can wait. That's what I wanted to share with you. Anyhow, the show must go on and I am with you in prayer," she said with what little energy she could muster.

"Thank you Rebeccah so much," he said with a cracking voice concerned for the virtuous woman on the phone that he was falling in love with.

"It's not a problem."

There was so much more she needed to say and ask him, but her mouth would not open to let them form or come out. *If it's your will Lord I will be silent.* "Brian, everything will be fine," was the only thing that she was able to say. Her heart wished for more but her anger and ego wanted to rebel and curse him out because the man could have known who Brian was. Something calming came over her. She felt that it was Brian's soothing voice but then realized that maybe it was the Lord. *Lord is this how your presence feels.*

"That it will, Rebeccah. When all of this is over today, I feel in my spirit that you and I need to talk. Do you mind if I come through later on when everything is finished here?"

"I don't mind at all," she said still taken aback by what she was feeling.

"Ok, I will see you then. Someone is calling me for Bible study so I will be there when I can."

"Ok, and thank you again, Brian. As we say in show business break a leg," she tried to crack a little joke but knew that it was inappropriate.

"I'll try not to. Just playing. Thank you and you are in my prayers," he said trying to put her at ease but wanting to tell her that he loved her.

"And so are you," she replied. "Bye."

"Bye," he said not wanting to hang up.

Rebeccah did not know why she was not able to say the things that were heavy on her mind but something was pulling her away from the wrong thoughts and kept her at peace. She was thankful again for whatever had taken control over her and hoped that she was not going crazy.

"Say Rebeccah, how are you feeling?" asked Kathy as

she walked into the room

"For some strange reason I am ok now," Rebeccah said in slight astonishment while looking up at her friend who was now sitting next to her.

"I made some breakfast for us and I am so thankful for cable girl because we can still watch the sermon without having to be at church today," Kathy said in what little excitement she could pull together. Kathy was hoping her friend would be able to tolerate being able to at least watch the service on television in her emotional condition.

"What do you mean?"

"It's a live broadcast, girl."

"Funny, I didn't know that," Rebeccah said while thinking how it was a good idea that she didn't go to church in her condition because everyone would have been able to see exactly how she felt; abused.

"Yeah, girl," Kathy said gently nudging her friend on the shoulder. "The service will be on at 10:00."

"You mean my big head would have been on television today if I was there?"

"But of course," she stated while rubbing her friends head, "and your head is not that big."

Rebeccah looked at Kathy a little off knowing that the first thing Kathy would always say to her was *good morning bighead* or *girl you know you got a big head*. It brought a little smile to Rebeccah's face.

"Ok maybe just a little, but still you are beautiful," she grabbed her best friends hand to get her off of the bed and led her into the living room. "So lets go eat some breakfast, bighead."

"See you are not right," Rebeccah said while grinning. She even made an attempt to even gather together a little laugh.

"Are you going to make it ok?" Kathy asked noticing that her friend was moving a little awkward from the pain.

"Yes I am," she paused, "by the way Kathy."

"Yes, girl?'

"Thank you for being here and being a part of my life," she said nervously.

"No problem that's what sisters in Christ do for one another."

It was a little ironic but Rebeccah didn't think of herself as a woman of God. She figured she was evolving into a woman for the Lord, even through her personal battle and what had happened to her the night before.

"Girl, I made some ham and eggs and then we have grits," Kathy said while pointing out the huge spread that she made for just the two of them. "I also put together some waffles and some mixed fruit. I wasn't sure If you were hungry or not."

Rebeccah looked at the entire meal on the table and thought that it would be better if she just had some grits, a little fruit, and a small piece of ham. "You shouldn't have gone to the extremes like you did for me, Kathy."

"It is too much, huh?" she stated while noticing that she may have over done it.

"Just a little," Rebeccah said feeling full just by looking at the spread. "But it all looks good."

"Well, I wasn't sure what you wanted so I kind of…" Kathy noticed that Rebeccah was a little shaken. "Girl, why are you crying? I'm sorry if I did something wrong."

"You didn't do anything wrong at all. Matter of fact, everything you have done now seems right. I don't know how to explain what I am feeling but all I can say is, thank you."

"Like I said sweetie, everything is okay now," she said reassuring her best friend. "That's what I am here for."

"Thank you again," while no longer holding back her tears and looking up at the ceiling. "Lord, thank you."

"Just have a seat, Reebie. I'll put together a plate for you. I have the television set on channel twelve," she said while guiding her friend to the sofa. "Just sit here and I will get what you want."

Oh dear God, Rebeccah thought. The emotions that were running through her were even more overwhelming than when she was on the phone with Brian. *I know that you are here to guide me. Thank you for guiding me Father.*

"Here's some tissue and a glass of juice," Kathy said handing her the items. "What would you like to eat?"

"Girl, whatever you put on my plate I will enjoy it."

With that, Kathy fixed her a plate which was ironically not piled high with everything that was on the table. It was if she had read Rebeccah's mind. She fixed her a bowl of grits with just enough sugar and butter. There was also a small plate of fruit with a portion of ham. Rebeccah wanted to cry at the site of how her friends had come to her aid just when she needed it the most. Instead of crying, that previous calming feeling came over her again and guided her to eat her meal.

"Oh girl," Kathy said excitedly which happened to startle Rebeccah for a quick second and pointing to the television. "Here it is. Look at Terrence up there. That's mah boy! Work that choir, brotha."

Rebeccah noticed that Kathy was right and that Terry was working the choir. They didn't talk much while the choir was performing and watching Terry on the television. She never knew how handsome her friend was until they panned up and did a close up of him. To this day she did not know why he had given up on the idea of being with a woman. He would have made a perfect husband for any woman. She figured that maybe something had happened to him in his childhood that forced him to be the way and live the life that he currently lived. She wondered if she would change her style of living after all that happened. The thought even crossed her mind that maybe she would no longer be suitable for any man and would force her into becoming gay for being afraid of being touched by male hands again. *Will I doubt my ability to be with a man after this? What man will even want me after all is said and done.*

"Girl, look at Brian" Kathy pointed to the Television and bringing Rebeccah out of her thoughts. "I mean Pastor up there in his robe."

Rebeccah had been so caught up in her thinking that she was unaware that Brian was walking up to the pulpit about to preach. In her eyes he was handsome, but a certain part of her had doubts, not about his past but about who the man was that had attacked her and how did he know Brian, if he knew him. She set aside her plate and juice and placed her elbows on her knees. Brian's demeanor and his presence on screen had Rebeccah's complete attention. She was sure he was able to move a crowd but she wanted to see if she could read his every move just to see if he had some inclination as to what had happened. She had to have answers.

"I'd like to thank all of you for being with us here today at The Holy Tabernacle of God," Brian said. "We would like to extend a welcome to you today. But not just today, our doors are always open for you everyday. You know I have been studying for this day. Seeing that this is my first revival that I have had here with The Holy Tabernacle of God, and I had my lesson planned out. But right now something is heavier on my spirit that I can not shake."

There were a few people in the audience saying their amen's in agreement.

"I hope you don't mind this morning."

"That's alright, pastor," a few people said in the background.

It was really touching for Rebeccah to see him in the pulpit. She had learned so much from him, especially during their Bible studies they would have over the phone. For a split second Rebeccah could see herself being with him for the rest of her life. She didn't know where the thought came from but she was proud to see him there demanding and courageous.

"Now, I want you all to be patient with me here in the church, and to those of you who are watching our live broadcast here on channel twelve. My spirit is telling me that what I had planned for is not the sermon I need to preach about on today."

"That's alright," a woman's voice said.

"You know when the spirit leads you, you have to follow and obey the Lords word. Set aside yourself, what ego you may have, and let the Lord direct you where you need to go. Give Him who is all, knows all, and is above all the-the power to lead you and guide you. Can I get an amen?"

"Amen," the congregation said in unison.

"That's right, Amen Preacher," Kathy said as if she were sitting there in church herself. Rebeccah didn't even pay attention to her. Her mind and concentration was set on the television and the image of the man who had just a few days prior asked to be in a relationship with her.

"I was going to preach today about the Book of Hosea but right now, right now is not the time," Brian said while looking back for agreement behind him from one of the guest Preachers.

"Alright now," a guest Preacher said while clapping his hands.

"Instead, I want to talk to you about something much different. The Lord is guiding me today saying that there is someone right here and right now that, that someone needs to know this. So I am going to do just that. Can I get an amen this morning somebody?"

"Amen," a few people said in the background.

"Our subject for today is this, Where is my Faith? With a subtext of how do I maintain my faith? Where is my Faith and how do I maintain my Faith?"

"Preach on Preacher," another guest Preacher said.

"Does everyone have his or her Bibles with them today," Brian looked around to see if everyone had a Bible in the church while holding his up in his hand. "Hold them up. That's right, let's see those wanting to be closer to the Lord. For those of you who do not have one share with your neighbor because this is about to be worth your while."

Brian sat his Bible back down on the podium and wiped his forehead with his handkerchief.

"Those of you out there in television land have your Bible ready, too," Brian said while looking directly at the camera.

Without looking over, Rebeccah could tell that Kathy was going through her Bible as if she were at the church ready to learn like the rest of the parishioners.

"Do you want to share with me?" Kathy asked glancing over at Rebeccah.

"Nah, girl," Rebeccah said not taking her eyes off of the television. "That's okay. I just want to hear what he has to say."

"The Greek word for faith in the New Testament is *pistis* meaning faith, trust, or truthfulness," he began to say while looking through his notes for some sort of encouragement. "The Greek verb for faith is *pisteuo* meaning, I trust or believe. In the Old Testament, *amen,* this means reliability or stability. Today however, we will be using the New Testament version, I believe or I trust."

"Say it with me I believe and I trust," Brian was looking directly into the camera once again. "That's right, amen."

"Now turn your Bibles to James 1: 2-8. While you are looking up James 1 verses 2 through 8, I also want you to mark or write down somewhere Chapter two verses fourteen through twenty-six. If everyone who has it, say Amen," he said while looking for acknowledgement.

"Amen," the audience said as the camera panned out

showing people going through their Bibles.

"James 1:2-8," he again repeated and then took a sip of water.

Rebeccah was looking intently while Kathy was writing down the verses.

"The History of the Epistle of James is that he was addressed as a servant of God," he began after he sat down his glass of water. "He was writing the letter to the twelve tribes, and portions of the verses were addressed to the nonbelievers of Christ. James one verses two through eight reads as follows in New King James Version *My brethren, count it all joy when you fall into various trials, knowing that the testing of your faith produces patients. But let patience have its perfect work, that you may be perfect and complete, lacking nothing.*"

Rebeccah was wondering if Brian was talking directly to her because while he was reading, he would look directly into the camera. She knew that the television separated them, but she felt as if he was speaking only to her. '*Count it all joy when you fall into carious trials, knowing that the testing of your faith produces patients.*'

"Is this what this is all about, Lord?" she said to herself. "This test that I have been placed in of being raped, is this what I am suppose to learn, to be patient?" Rebeccah had always heard the old folk say that whatever dilemma or drama they had gone through in their life was blamed on the devil. "Oh chile you know that devil was the reason for my downfall," or "I am just of flesh, so there are times when I get tempted." Somehow after hearing what Brian had just read she felt that the true translation of what they could have been going through in reality was a test, tested by the Lord to see how faithful one truly says that they are and how truly they believe in Him.

"'*Abraham believed God, and it was accounted to him for righteousness' And he was called the friend of God.*' You see here then that the man is justified by works, and not just by faith alone," he said while turning the pages of his Bible once again.

"That's right, Preacher," someone said in the crowd.

"Keep talking, keep talking," one of the guest Preachers said.

"Now, I want you to write down Ephesians 1 verse 15 through twenty three," Brian said again looking into the crowd. "We won't have time to go over those but in your own time, read them. Ephesians 1 verses 15 through 23 explains what you will gain once you trust and have faith in God. He justifies and Sanctifies through faith in Galatians 3: 1-5 and 5: 25."

Rebeccah felt a chill come over her but did not move. She still sat in the same position she was in when she had started watching Brian. She was so content on not letting go of any of his words that she didn't even think to right down any of the Bible verse. On the other hand, Kathy was taking notes and marking everything down that Brian had mentioned. Rebeccah could tell that she was a true woman for Christ.

"Now in Hebrews chapter 11 verse one it reads as follows, but again the entire chapter is one you must study when you get the time. It reads as follows, Hebrews chapter 11 verse one, *'Now faith is the substance of things hoped for, the evidence of things not seen.'* In Christians and non-believers this gives us reassurance that God does what He says He is going to do. Through His promises, the faithful are reassured that God is always there through the trials and tribulations; through the hurt, hunger, and pain. From being a battered wife, a homeless child, or a neglected child, God is there through it all. Can I get an amen today?"

Everyone began saying their amen's, some even began clapping.

"*'Now faith is the substance of things hoped for, the evidence of things not seen.'* I don't know what it is that you have gone through, and I don't know what it is that you have been placed in, but what I do know is that my God can move mountains. My God can reach me when I feel like I am not able to be reached."

Some of the audience began to shout. Rebeccah found herself rocking back in forth in her seat.

"If I have a problem in my life, my faith for my God brings me back to let me know that I am thankful for each and every trial that He places me in. I am thankful for being brought up the way I was when no one knew my sorrows but Him. I am thankful for who He has made me become today. Whatever it is that is troubling you thank God for it because He is still the Alpha and the Omega. Believe that if He is placing His child through the trails, even though it hurts Him to see the pain, He will still be there if you just call on Him."

Tears began streaming down Rebeccah's face. The audience was still captivated by what Brian was saying because the camera panned out a second time to show people standing on their feet and shouting.

"Just like a mother watches her child trying to walk or goes off to school for the very first time, it hurts to let go, but the end result, Hallelujah," Brian sang while looking directly at the camera, "the end result is more glorious than the trials that you go through. That child trust and believes that when he or she gets off that bus, his mother will be there, regardless of how the day went at school. If little Billy or Kiki got beat up at school, they know that their mother will be right there never doubting that she will leave them abandoned. She will stand there with open arms and a smile, accepting them for who they are."

By then Rebeccah could not hold herself anymore. Her rocking had gotten even stronger; her tears were falling even harder and faster. She had to hold herself because she knew that all that she had gone through was just a trial. The pain hurt, but for her to know that there would be something better coming for her at the end of the day was much better. So much so that all she could do was shout, "thank you Lord. Thank You for being with me when I feel that there is no one else to look to but You. I trust You with my life, even though I felt You turned Your back on me. Forgive me for not believing that You are my Father for all these years. You have been there for me wanting me to come back to Your loving arms. I slid away from You, but all You ever wanted and asked of me was to be there for You."

Kathy was fanning her friend but Rebeccah didn't even notice. Both of them were crying but something remained in Rebeccah's spirit. She knew what she had to do. That was to dedicate her life to Christ.

Chapter
12

"Pastor Foster, thank you for that sermon today," Lesha said trying to get closer to Brian. "I really needed it."

"You're welcome, Sister Walker," he said while trying to get to his office. He only had Rebeccah on his mind and in his heart and the obstacle that was standing in his way was not going to stop him.

"We all need a little faith in our lives," she grinned.

"Yes ma'am, Sister, that we do," he said as he was still trying to ease by her but she just kept following him.

He really didn't have the time to speak with her. He had something else on his mind; he was worried about no one or nothing but Rebeccah. He knew that when he was preaching the sermon that those words were not words of his own. He knew that the spirit worked through him because his plan was to talk about the church and how present day churches related to Hosea and his bride. He figured he wasn't supposed to speak about it and followed what the Lord gave him. While walking through the hallway and greeting people headed towards his office, he could only think of Rebeccah and her smile. Ever since he stepped down from the pulpit, seeing Rebeccah was the only thing he knew he needed to do next. He had so many other plans for the day. Different preachers had come into town that he had personally invited, for the revival. He felt he needed to slip away for a minute just to go by her house and see her. Brian had to explain to the guest Preachers that he needed to step out for a minute and they understood completely. Lesha was still standing by him the entire time. The Mission committee had cooked up a meal for the Preachers. He felt that they would not miss him just for a few minutes. He realized that Lesha had followed him to his car.

"Uhm excuse me, sister," he said finally looking at Lesha. "I need to leave out and I don't want to bump you with my car door."

"Oh I'm sorry," she said looking a little confused and upset. "Why are you leaving? You have a church to look out for. There's no need to go see her."

Lesha stopped herself because she realized what she was about to say and looked off. As she looked away, Brian had a look of curiosity towards Lesha. He felt something wasn't right.

"Excuse me," he said looking at her still with curiosity and a bit of anger. "You know... not right now Sister and not with you. I will talk to you at another time."

"Whatever," she smartly replied. "She aint nothing anyway. She just used up by now."

Brian didn't want to hear her babble on, so he got into his car and drove off. He could still see Lesha standing where he left her through his rearview mirror. He figured how shameful some women look and how far they go just to get the attention they want. He contemplated a minute on what she said about Rebeccah being used up. It was a strange comment to say the least, coming from her. Brian wondered how much Lesha knew about Rebeccah. He then brushed it off because he didn't want to be bothered with Lesha anymore.

It had taken him about five minutes to get to Rebeccah's condo. She stayed in a nice district that had been revitalized in downtown Tennessee. It was a very high upscale community. While he was driving, he could imagine himself living in the area. He pulled up to the front of the building and as he was getting out of his car, he gave the keys to the valet. He couldn't help but think about how nice of a life it would be with Rebeccah. His little one bedroom apartment was nice, but where she stayed felt like home. He walked by the doorman, the security desk, and then to the elevator. They didn't stop him because they had seen him come around on several afternoons to meet with Rebeccah. The young man at the desk spoke to him while he was waiting for the elevator.

"Have a good day, sir," he said as the doors opened.

"Thank you," said Brian while he was thinking of how wonderful his life would be if he lived in the building with Rebeccah. "Yup! I could do this for a while," he whispered under his breath while the elevator went to her floor.

He had a funny feeling because he was concerned about the woman he cared for. They hadn't officially announced that they been dating but he was going to take their relationship to the next level after service. He wanted to announce to the entire guest Preachers that she was his girlfriend and they were going to need a mentor to prep them for dating in the eyes of the Lord. The elevator finally made it to the 10th floor penthouse. No matter how many times Brian had visited Rebeccah, he was always amazed at how much class she had. He wanted to have her by his side for a long time as Mrs. Rebeccah Elise Foster.

Brian rushed to the door and didn't think about ringing the doorbell.

Knock-knock.

He could hear someone on the other side looking through the peep whole.

"Its pastor Foster," Kathy said while opening the

door. "What is he doing here he should be at church. Girl, do you want me to let him in?"

Brian waited patiently for her to answer but Kathy's voice had faded away from the door and he heard several locks come undone.

"Uhm, hello is Rebeccah here," he said not realizing that it was Rebeccah standing in front of him. "Oh my God baby, what happened to you? Are you okay?"

All he saw standing before him was Rebeccah bruised up in some baggy sweat pants and a hoodie over her head. He reached up almost wanting to touch the bruised side of her face but didn't want to over step his boundaries. He noticed her eyes were swollen and blood shot red as if she had a rough fight the night before. He knew from what Terry had told him that something was wrong but he didn't know it was as serious as it looked. He wanted to hold her and to comfort her, but something kept holding him back.

"I'm ok," she said looking at him then looking down. "Come in."

She didn't want him to see her in her current shape; she wanted him to see her as she was when he first met her. She covered that woman up, the one who had the attitude, fancy car, homes, and everything that was worldly. Then she thought that maybe the woman that was now standing before him was the one that she truly was. One who had to go through a battle with all the scars in order for her to change and to be a new woman in Christ. Rebeccah looked over at Kathy who had gotten the hint to give the two of them some time alone. Brian walked in as he closed the door behind him.

"I am going to leave you two alone," Kathy said while looking to see if her friend would be ok. "Call me if you need anything."

"Thanks, girl. I will," she said as she waited for her to go into the guest bedroom. "Have a seat. Would you uhm like something to drink or eat?"

Rebeccah looked over to the table as if it were the only escape that she would have from not allowing Brian to see her in her as she was.

"No I'm fine," he said as he had sat down. His heart was saying to her that he loved her and his eyes were filled with concern. He wanted to know who had hurt her but he waited for Rebeccah to speak.

"I uhm," she gulped trying not to seem scared. "I heard your sermon on channel twelve. I really think you were speaking to me at the…"

"I was just being a vessel doing what I was told to do," he said trying to make her feel at ease.

"Well it was worth hearing," she said looking into his eyes and then looking back down. "Especially now."

"Like I told you over the phone, I am here for you whenever you need me," he said as he reached out to hold her hand.

"Aren't you supposed to be at church?" she asked as she slowly moved her hand away from his. She noticed that he had a sad look on his face. He could tell that she was a little uncomfortable so he didn't force the issue. *Lord please guide me right now, please I will be your faithful servant.*

"I am, but I told them that I had a family emergency," he said still wanting to know who hurt her.

"Family, huh?" she said with a grin that she could muster up.

"Yeah, well you are part of my family, and the churches family."

"Hhm! that sounds strange, a church family. I wanted to talk to you about that, too."

"Sure go ahead."

"I wanted to, when I get a little better, I wanted to dedicate my life to Christ. I know that I was young and all when I was first baptized but now I feel I need to do something."

"What better time than today, that is if you are up to it?"

"No I am not up to it right now but, I do want to when I get a little better."

"If you don't mind me asking," he couldn't hold it in much longer, "baby, what happened?"

It felt good inside to her hearing him call her baby as gentle as he did for the first time. She wanted to be held but was afraid and still a little confused. "I don't mind you asking. I felt I needed to approach you with this first before I took it to anyone else. I didn't even tell the cops anything yet. Something told me to come to you first."

"Well, I'm here now."

"And I thank you for being here, too. Brian, I need to know something and I want you to be honest."

"Okay."

"Did you put someone up to this?"

"Did I do what," he asked in shock and disbelief. "Why would I do that?"

"I figured you may know the person who did this to me."

"Why would you think that?"

"Because, he said your name a couple of times."

"Are you sure he said my name?"

"Yes he did, and what hurts the most is I don't want to believe that you knew this guy."

"I can't say that I do, Reebie. I was still at church yesterday and then went over to one of the sister's house because she and her husband sponsored some of the out of town Preachers. It couldn't have been me."

"I was hoping you would say that," she said with a sigh of relief. "But this guy seemed to really know you."

"Is it too much for me to ask you to start from the beginning, or at least to the point where you feel comfortable?"

She took a deep breath and began telling Brian everything from her sitting at her office to being in the hospital. She even told him about being raped. There was a look of anger in his eyes along with tears. She could tell that he felt her pain and knew that she was just doing her work and not bothering anyone. She was not like the girls that he knew back in the day, she was his virtuous woman.

"You said this guy who attacked you said that, and I know this is hard for you because this is hard for me too, but he said that you have come into my life and that you took me away from him and the life that I once knew?"

"Uh huh," she shook her head in agreement.

"And what did this guy look like?"

"I don't know, he had some kind of mask over his head but I do know that he had a tattoo on his neck shaped like a scorpion."

Brian's eyes had gotten big and he filled up with anger. He had a feeling of who it was but he didn't want it to be true. He couldn't understand why he would do anything to Rebeccah because she was not the reason for him changing his life. It was just time for him to move forward, especially after the last vacation he had taken with him to San Diego.

"Is everything okay?" Rebeccah asked noticing that Brian was upset.

"Yeah everything is fine," he said and then flashed back to what Lesha had told him in the church parking lot before he made it to Rebeccah's house. The entire thing had Brian thinking and his anger was telling him that he needed to do something right away. He first wanted to console Rebeccah. "Rebeccah, I uhm, think I might know who the guy is."

"What?" she shockingly replied. She could hear something fall in her guest bedroom but she didn't turn her head to see because she felt a little disappointed in what she was hearing. "You may know who it is?"

"Yeah but Rebeccah, I want you to know that I had nothing, nothing at all to do with this. I do know how to make this right though."

"What! What are you going to do?"

"Don't worry, babygirl. I can take control of this. I have protected myself all this time. I can't let a man and his ignorance mess with my lady, not like this. This isn't supposed to be this way."

"Don't do anything crazy," she said as Kathy was rushing into the room. "You still have to go back to church."

"Nah! Right now Rebeccah this is not about church," he said as he rushed out the door.

As Brian got into the elevator he could not believe how his so called friend could do something so violating to Rebeccah. This man was supposed to be his best friend. Brian didn't want to leave out the way he did, but he felt he needed to settle this ordeal once and for all. She was going to be the woman that he would be with for the rest of his life. He realized that this no good for nothing sorry excuse of a man had taken what did not belong to him. What made it worse was the man threatened her with a gun. Brian bet that Lesha had a hand in all that had happened. He bet his life on it. First he needed to make a stop at his apartment and pick up his protection then head over to the old neighborhood where he knew Mike would be.

"Oh God why did I tell Brian?" Rebeccah said under her breath. She figured that by the way he left out of her house there would be more drama which she felt she didn't need more of. *Why am I being tested like this, Lord?*

"Reebie, is everything okay?" Kathy asked.

"I told Brian what had happened, and he rushed out."

"Don't be mad at me, but I heard."

"You heard what part?"

"All of it!'"

Rebeccah could have been upset with her but by the way she was feeling she was concerned with what Brian had planned on doing. She couldn't help but just fall down on her knees in the middle of the floor and start crying.

"Reebie, it's going to be okay," Kathy said while she started rubbing her friend's shoulders to console her.

"No it's not. This is my fault! I should have told the police this morning when I had a chance, that way they could have gotten the guy before Brian stormed out of here. Now he is going to jeopardize his career over this, I don't want this in my life?"

"Reebie, but it is going to be okay."

"Stop saying that! Its not!"

"No, but it is. I have friends in high places, too" Kathy said while looking to the sky asking God to watch over all that was about to happen.

Chapter
13

And a time for every purpose under heaven…

"See this fool right here thinks he's slick," Brian said while pulling up to his old stomping grounds. It had taken him a few minutes to get to his house. He did have at least one last call to make, which was to Mama Jenkins to let her know that he would be a little late and that things came up. He also asked her if she could get one of the guest Preachers to preach for the evening service. Church was the last thing on his mind. He had revenge and he wanted to show that he no longer needed to have his boy in his life. "How in the hell, excuse me, Lord," he whispered, "but how in the hell could a man like that do that to a helpless woman and to prove his point to me?"

The more Brian thought about what his boy did, they angrier he had gotten. He put his Bible in the backseat, took off his cross, rolled up his car windows, and turned off the car. "Oh see there go that Negro right now," he said as his eyes and face began to burn with heat.

Mike had walked out of the corner package store and stood on the corner. Brian got out of the car and started walking towards him.

"Ayo Mike, hold up man."

"Ahh Preacher boy callin' himself coming back to the

hood. They aint doing you right at the church, huh? I told you that life wasn't for you man, you need to be back home with us."

Brian ran up on Mike and socked him in his jaw.

"Oh so now you want to be rough guy," Mike said while rubbing his jaw. "Yeah see that's what I am talking about. I knew the hood was still in you."

"Man how could you do this, man? You *was* my boy."

"Do what? oh," he said trying to act like he could not recall. "You mean that bitch? She deserved it."

Sock.

He hit him again the next time for calling Rebecca out of her name and for admitting that he hurt her. People on the street stopped to watch while others looked out of their windows. "A man, whatever beef you had between me you, you could have told me," Brian said looking angry.

"Don't get your suit all ruined brah, she wasn't even worth it man," Mike said acting disgusted.

"I should hit you again for even thinking about touching her."

"Look here, niggah. This is my neck of the woods now. You left us a long time ago, Preacher boy."

"But that still does not give you the right to hurt her. If you had beef with me you should have said something man. I thought we was boys."

"You thought? You thought, niggah. You left your boy a long time ago after you finished school and left me behind. You got with that sadity chick and forgot about where you came from. Besides, I did that as a favor for you."

"A favor?!"

"Man, if them people knew what you was about when you was running the streets, they wouldn't want you around anymore. I did this for you to protect you."

"You can't protect me man, you aint God."

"See, that's where you wrong," he said as he pulled

out his gun and pointed it to Brian's forehead. "Now see who is God, niggah. Preacher can't even talk now. Look at him all scared and shit. Who you goin' to ask for now? You can't ask God 'cause he aint here holding this here gun. He aint here with his finger on the trigger. I am."

"Man, I aint goin' out like no punk, man," Brain said and pulled out his nine from behind his back.

"See that's the boy I know," Mike said smiling as if he was encouraging Brian. "Come back to this side man. You know we need you back, man. We got nothing but love for you here; they got nothing but lies and pain. She wasn't worth it no way, man she wasn't..."

Pop-pop the sound rang in his ears.

"Oh my God he got shot," someone yelled.

That was the last thing Brian remembered hearing in the background as he began to fall to the ground.

Epilogue

The amount of people sitting in the courtroom was quiet anxiously awaiting the verdict. If a mouse were to scamper across the floor, now would be the time to notice. As the jury sat in the stand, not noticing the onlookers, the bailiff handed the judge the piece of paper with following eyes from all. The answer that everyone waited on was on that one tiny piece of paper that could take away a lifetime of hope for one. The written words that had taken the jury over two weeks to decide on was now in the hands of the man that would allow all to know the truth, or the lie. The judge nodded his head to the bailiff while his glasses sat on the rim of his nose taking his precious time before opening up the piece of paper that could hold all the answers for one. Each unfolding of the note had everyone holding their breath even longer frightened for what was to come. He looked down at the note twice up at the jurors then back at the note once again. He looked up one last time to make sure he had seen each of the jurors face to see if they were all on one accord with their decision. Once approved by not seeing much but eyes looking down unsure and away, he folded the note and handed it back to the Bailiff. The bailiffs steps back to the head juror seemed to take several minutes due to the anticipation, but in reality time was not in slow motion one bit. He passed the note to the head juror and then walked away.

"Have you all come to an agreement with your decision?" asked the judge.

"Yes, we have your honor," the jury foreman answered.

"What say you in the decision of the defendant?"

"We the jury find the defendant guilty on all counts."

From the answer, everyone in the courthouse

jumped up and hollered.

"Order in the court! Order in the court!" the judge said hitting the gavel to gain order of his courtroom. "If you all do not be quiet I will have to send each and every one of you out."

The judge looked around to see if everyone was in agreement with him and that they would not make another sound.

"On the count of murder in the first degree, what do you call? "

"We the jury find the defendant guilty as charged."

"In the county of Davidson, and in the state of Tennessee, we will set judging for the defendant in two weeks. If nothing further court's adjourned."

The sound of the gavel hitting against the wood and the noise of the onlookers frightened the defendant. The accused turned around to see who was in the courtroom thinking, "where is that one face that always eases my spirit?"

Book Club Questions from Shani Fenderson

Do you think you have an idea to the ending?

1. Did Brian die? If so, who do you think did it?

2. Who do you think was sitting in the courthouse looking for that face that always eased the person's spirit?

3. What do you like/dislike about Reebie? Brian? Mike? Sister Walker?

4. How does Ecclesiastics play into the last few chapters?

5. Was Brian ready for true love? Why or why not?

6. Do you think Reebie has found inner peace? Why or why not?

7. Why do you feel it was hard for Brian to let go of his past (going to the club in San Diego, staying at her house, carrying a gun, the urge to kill)?

8. On a lighter note; will you try any of the recipes? If you do, please be sure to leave me a note on www.shanifenderson.com and let me know how you enjoyed it. I look forward to your responses.

All of your answers to the questions above will be in the next novel *To Be*. God bless you all and thank you for your support.

Follow Shani Fenderson on Twitter:
www.twitter.com/maylodi and Facebook for more answers.
www.facebook.com/mayhousepress

Be sure to check out more
From
Shani Fenderson

Mommy Why is the Sky So Blue?

978-1-60749-550-5

Solitaire: A Love Story

978-1604411225

What's next
from
Shani Fenderson

*Evolution of a Woman
To Be*

Visit Shani Fenderson at www.shanifenderson.com
You may also purchase additional books at Barnes and
Nobles.com or Amazon.com.